"As far as I'm concerned, Bart Reed is all yours!" announced Caroline.

"As long as I pretend to be you," Chrissy reminded her with a giggle.

But Caroline's face was serious. "We can't let anyone know what we are planning," she warned her cousin. "We can't even tell any of our friends about it. We can't take any chances."

Chrissy giggled. "I feel like we are planning some sort of secret mission. Operation: Blind Date. This date will self-destruct at the stroke of midnight on Friday."

Caroline smiled. "We'll just tell all our friends that I have a date for Friday night and you are planning on closeting yourself all evening to catch up on some studying."

"And if I happen to see anyone we know while I'm at the ballet with Bart, I'll just hide behind the seats in front of us," Chrissy replied confidently. But inside, her stomach flipped over. Could she really trick Bart into believing she was Caroline?

Other books in the **SUGAR & SPICE** series:

COMING SOON

Janet Quin-Harkin's

Sugar & Spice

Blind Date

IVY BOOKS • NEW YORK

To Carla Bracale

Ivy Books
Published by Ballantine Books
Copyright © 1988 by Butterfield Press, Inc. & Janet Quin-Harkin

Produced by Butterfield Press, Inc.
133 Fifth Avenue
New York, New York 10003

Library of Congress Catalog Card Number: 87-92087

ISBN 0-8041-0094-2

Manufactured in the United States of America

First Edition: June 1988

Chapter 1

Caroline Kirby awoke slowly, pulled from her pleasant dreams by the familiar sounds of San Francisco drifting in through the open bedroom window. She snuggled down deeper beneath the lightweight bed covers, a soft smile curving her lips. There was nothing nicer than waking up on a beautiful March morning, with a cool breeze carrying in the salty aroma from the bay below. From outside the window, she could hear the clanging of cable-car bells and loud blasts of ship horns from the bay—all the comforting sounds of home that had awakened her nearly every morning for as long as she could remember. Her blue eyes suddenly flew open as she realized that the noises she had more recently grown accustomed to hearing every morning were glaringly

1

absent. She turned over and eyed her clock radio, frowning as she saw that the digital numbers read 9:03. Her gaze slowly shifted to the bed on the opposite side of the bedroom. The lump beneath the covers and the jumble of blond hair peeking out from the top of the blanket were the only signs that attested to the fact that Chrissy was still in bed. Caroline's frown deepened. After nine o'clock on a beautiful Saturday morning and Chrissy was still in bed? Having been raised on a farm in Iowa, Chrissy was used to rising with the roosters. And even though there were no roosters in San Francisco, Chrissy had brought her farm hours with her. Only occasionally did she sleep late, even on a weekend.

Caroline opened her mouth to call to her cousin, then stopped herself. *As Mom says, don't look a gift horse in the mouth,* she thought to herself. *Take advantage of the unusual peace and quiet! Peace and quiet.* She smiled once again, and closed her eyes with a contented sigh. There had been very little peace and quiet in her life since Chrissy had come to San Francisco the summer before last. Whether being escorted home by a fire engine, or skiing down an expert slope her very first time on snow skis, Chrissy threw herself into life with all the exuberance of a kid at a carnival.

Never in her wildest dreams could Caroline have imagined a cousin like Chrissy. When she'd met Chrissy for the first time at the airport, Caroline had expected a shy, timid girl—but she couldn't have been more wrong! Chrissy had talked a blue streak from the very first moment, and had rarely stopped talking ever since. At times, Caroline was embarrassed by Chrissy's unpolished country ways, but secretly she admired her cousin's outrageous sense of adventure.

Now Caroline turned over once again to face the lump in the bed across the room. Usually, by seven o'clock in the morning Chrissy was out of bed, trying to sneak quietly into the bathroom, but in the process making enough noise to wake up everyone in the building. Worry darkened Caroline's eyes, and she pushed a strand of her blond hair behind her ear. Was it possible that Chrissy was ill? Caroline's frown deepened once again as she wondered what to do.

"Chrissy?" she finally called hesitantly across the room. There was no answer. "Chrissy?" The lump beneath the covers didn't even move. "Chrissy, are you awake?" she called a little louder.

"Hhrumph," the lump grunted in reply.

"Chrissy, are you feeling all right? I mean, are you sick or something?" Caroline looked at the lump with concern.

"Holy Mazoly, Cara!" Chrissy flopped the blankets down to the end of the bed and sat up, her blue eyes sparkling merrily. "Here I am, practicing real self-control, lying as quietly as a church mouse during Sunday services, figuring I'd give you a break this morning—and then you wake up wagging your jaws like laundry on a clothesline flapping in the wind!"

Caroline giggled at her cousin's outburst and rolled over on her back, fluffing up the pillow beneath her head. "So, what's the occasion? I don't think I've ever seen you as quiet as a church mouse."

Chrissy shrugged and tried to smooth down her sleep-tousled blond hair. "I knew you were out pretty late last night with Francis, so I thought you might appreciate a little extra snooze time this morning."

Caroline looked at her cousin with a pained expression. "Chrissy, his name is François, not Francis. It's French."

Chrissy raised her pale eyebrows. "Well, excuse *moi!* Did you have a good time?"

"It was all right," Caroline said without enthusiasm.

"Just all right?" Chrissy asked, folding her long legs up under her in Indian fashion. "But, you and he seemed to have so many things in common. You seemed so perfect for each other."

"I know," Caroline replied. She sat up, and drew her knees to her chest. "When François asked me out for last night, I was really hoping we'd have a lot to talk about. You know, we are in the same music appreciation class at school and we worked together on a French club committee last month." She sighed unhappily. "He is a very nice guy, but we just didn't click at all."

Chrissy looked at Caroline suspiciously. "This wouldn't have anything to do with a certain letter you got yesterday postmarked from Iowa, would it?"

Caroline nodded, her glum expression changing into a soft, dreamy look. "Oh, Chrissy, Luke sent me the sweetest, most wonderful letter yesterday. There are times when I miss him so much I could just cry!" She bit down on her bottom lip, her thoughts going back in time to last spring, when she had visited Chrissy's home in Danbury, Iowa. Caroline hadn't been thrilled about spending her spring break in Danbury, but that had been before she'd met Luke Masterson, a boy from the neighboring farm. Even now, after a full year since that trip, Caroline could not forget the magic of her time with Luke, the wonder and thrill of his kisses. She sighed again. "It seems to me like the more boys I date, the more I realize just how special Luke is."

"I remember when I felt the same way about Ben," Chrissy remarked. "I almost passed up the chance to come here because I didn't want to leave Ben in Danbury. And now, well, we just don't see eye to eye on things anymore. I hope long-distance love works out better for you than it did for me."

"I hope so, too. You know, I think Luke and I are destined to be together." Caroline glanced away from her cousin. "But right now it hurts so much being apart, and going out with François just reminded me of how much I miss Luke."

"At least you had a date last night," Chrissy continued. "It's been so darned long since I had a real date. I'm beginning to wonder if my breath smells like a garbage dump!"

Caroline giggled as Chrissy cupped her hand in front of her mouth and blew, then fell back on the bed in a mock faint. Chrissy cracked open an eyelid and grinned, pleased that she had been able to pull her cousin from her momentary doldrums. "Besides," Chrissy began, bounding off the bed with a burst of energy, "who needs boys and dating anyway?" She walked over to the bedroom window and threw it all the way open, allowing the salt-tinged breezes to ruffle her hair and flatten her nightgown against her body. She leaned far out of the window and took a deep, cleansing breath. "Think about it, Cara," she yelled, projecting her voice into the wind. "What do we need boys for. We could always be old maids with blue hair, and live together forever in a big, old house with twenty or thirty cats!"

"No way!" Caroline objected. "Chrissy, come away from that window!" Caroline blushed, wondering what on earth all the people down on the sidewalk below must be thinking about the girl hanging out the third-floor window. "Come on, Chrissy," she hissed in embarrassment. "You're in San Francisco, remember? Not Danbury."

"Ouch!" Chrissy yelped, banging her head on the window as she pulled herself back into the bedroom. "Well, I am just a country girl at heart.

Anyway, Cara, can't you imagine us as roommates at seventy years old?"

"Only in my nightmares." Caroline grinned. "Besides, you are much too big a slob for me to live with forever." She motioned to Chrissy's side of the room to emphasize her point.

Chrissy looked around, a sheepish expression crossing her face as she noticed the pile of dirty clothes on the floor, the homework strewn across the top of the dresser, an empty candy wrapper peeking out from under the bed. She drew herself up to her full height and looked at Caroline haughtily. "I may be a slob, but I am becoming a very cultured slob, dahling. And now, after you have so insulted me, I am going to go take my bath." She raised her nose snootily in the air, and began to walk out of the bedroom with studied elegance. It would have been a perfect exit had her big toe not hooked onto the belt loop of a pair of dirty jeans lying on the floor.

Caroline giggled merrily as Chrissy stumbled awkwardly, then righted herself and continued her exit, dragging the jeans along with her big toe. "Oh, Chrissy," Caroline giggled. "The day you become completely cultured is the day I will wrestle a pig!" Caroline fell back on her bed, laughter once again overcoming her.

Chapter 2

"Chrissy, what's the matter?" Caroline asked as she met her cousin outside Maxwell High the following Monday afternoon.

"Ah, nothing," Chrissy said in a small voice.

Caroline smiled gently. "Chrissy, your expression is about as difficult to read as a kindergarten book. Now, what is the matter?"

"This is the matter." Chrissy pulled a sheet of paper from her notebook and handed it to Caroline.

Caroline studied the paper for a moment, then handed it back to Chrissy. "Okay, you got a low grade on a senior lit paper. So you'll do better next time."

"That's easy for you to say," Chrissy replied glumly. She had known her cousin wouldn't really understand. Good grades came easily to Caroline. In fact, she had an excellent chance of getting a scholarship to college.

"Chrissy, it's just one grade in one class, not the end of the world," Caroline said gently.

"Yeah, but unfortunately there are more where that one came from." Chrissy sighed deeply. "Back in Danbury, grades weren't that important to me—and college, well, I'd never seriously thought about it. Now I've decided I definitely do want to go to college, but if I don't get some sort of a scholarship, I may as well forget it."

"You wouldn't need a scholarship to go to a community college," Caroline said softly.

"But Cara, I don't want to go to a community college. I want to go to a regular four-year college, like you," Chrissy declared. "I have been looking at those brochures you received from Colorado University in Boulder, and I think it all looks so neat. Oh, Cara, wouldn't it be wonderful if we both ended up going to the same college?" Chrissy's face beamed with excitement, then fell. "But I just know that won't happen. You will end up at some terrific big university and I'll end up in a two-year community college."

"Come on." Caroline dropped an arm around her cousin's shoulders sympathetically. "Let's forget about college for now. How about my treat at Mama's Ice Cream Store?"

Food always managed to lift Chrissy's spirits, and this time was no exception. "Can I order whatever I want?" she asked, her blue eyes sparkling once again.

"Anything on the menu," Caroline confirmed with a smile.

"Now, that is what I consider a great cousin!" Chrissy grinned happily, and together the two girls headed for Mama's Ice Cream Store.

It was an unusually warm spring day, and it seemed as if everyone else in San Francisco had been struck by the same sudden craving for ice cream. Chrissy and Caroline got their sundaes, then found an empty table in the corner of the crowded ice-cream parlor.

"Cara . . . Cara Kirby!"

Both girls looked around, trying to find the person who had called to Caroline.

"Cara . . . over here!"

This time Caroline and Chrissy spotted the thin, dark-haired girl squeezing through the crowd toward their table.

"Hi, Maddie!" Caroline greeted her friend, gesturing for her to join them. "Chrissy, this is Madeleine Walsh. Maddie and I were in Madame's ballet class together. Maddie, this is my cousin, Chrissy."

Chrissy smiled brightly at Madeleine, who gave a quick nod in her direction before turning back to Caroline. "Ballet class hasn't been the same since you dropped out, Cara. Madame is even more of a tyrant, if you can believe it. And don't you dare breathe a word of this little indulgence to anyone," she said, gesturing to the small ice-cream cone she held in her hand, "or Madame will have my head."

"Don't worry, that little-bitty ice-cream cone isn't really an indulgence," Chrissy scoffed in open friendliness. "Now this . . ." She looked down at her large dish of black-walnut ice cream topped with rich chocolate syrup and a gooey marshmallow-and-nut mixture. "This is true indulgence!"

"That is truly disgusting," Madeleine said, scrunching her nose in disapproval.

The smile on Chrissy's face wavered slightly. *She's just joking,* Chrissy assured herself, turning her attention back to her ice cream. *I don't think I'll ever get used to the dry sense of humor that some of these city kids think is cool. How could anyone seriously think this masterpiece is disgusting?* she wondered, taking another dripping spoonful of her sundae.

"You know how the infamous Madame is," Madeleine continued to Caroline. "Her beady little eyes can detect an extra ounce of weight on one of her dancers."

Caroline smiled sympathetically. "How well I remember." She looked down at her own large dish of ice cream, and Chrissy knew she was remembering all the treats she had denied herself in an effort to please the strict Madame.

Madeleine took a dainty lick of her ice cream. "Anyway, it must be ESP or something that I saw you here today. I was going to give you a call this evening."

"What a coincidence," Caroline said politely, but Chrissy could see that her cousin was curious.

"So, what have you been doing since you quit ballet?" Maddie asked, then continued without waiting for an answer. "Everyone was really shocked when you quit. You were so good—one of the best."

"Thanks, I miss everybody, too," Caroline said with a smile, a warm blush covering her cheeks. "But I just don't have the drive and the commitment it takes to be a dancer. All those sacrifices were too much for me."

"Tell me about sacrifices," Madeleine exclaimed, biting into her small cone with a crunch. "We're getting ready for Madame's spring recital now. She's been in a continuous rage for the past month, but you should see the beautiful costumes we get to wear this year!" Caroline smiled wistfully as Madeleine continued airily. "James says my costume makes me look like a Greek goddess. He's so sweet." She gave Caroline a pointed look. "Tell me, Cara, are you dating anyone special?"

Caroline hesitated for a moment, and Chrissy knew she was thinking about Luke, but she wasn't surprised when Caroline finally shook her head. Madeleine didn't seem like the kind of girl who would understand Caroline's attraction to a farm boy from Iowa who drove a dusty, old blue pickup truck and had a part-time job as a crop duster.

"No, I'm not dating anyone special," Caroline finally answered.

"Great, because that's what I wanted to talk to you about." Madeleine paused long enough to pop the last of her ice-cream cone into her mouth. "Last night at the club I met the most divine boy, and after talking to him for a while it suddenly struck me that you and he would be absolutely perfect for each other."

"What sort of club do you belong to?" Curiosity pulled the question out of Chrissy. She was always looking for new clubs to join, new interests to explore, new people to meet. "I've been thinking about joining one of those health clubs. You know, where you can work out and swim and stuff like that."

Madeleine looked at Chrissy with ill-concealed amusement. "Oh, really? Actually, I belong to the Pine Hills Country Club." She turned back to Caroline and continued. "Anyway, Bart, that's his name, Bart Reed, is a senior at the Forsythe School, and he is devastatingly handsome." She paused and looked at Caroline curiously. "Interested?"

"I don't know, Maddie," Caroline began hesitantly.

"But, Cara, you just have to meet him," Madeleine cut in smoothly. "Bart wants to be an arts journalist and I know your father does something like that, doesn't he?"

"Hmmm, Dad writes music reviews," Caroline answered without enthusiasm.

"And get this, Bart loves the ballet. In fact, he's really into the cultural scene. His parents are active patrons of the San Francisco Ballet, and Mrs. Reed does a lot of charity and fund-raising work. Your mother has probably met her."

"But Maddie . . ."

"I'm telling you, Cara, you and Bart are a match made in heaven. I've already told him all about you, and he's looking forward to meeting you." Madeleine smiled slyly. "As a matter of fact, I already gave him your phone number. He said he'd probably call you tonight around seven to ask you out for Friday night."

"Oh, Maddie, I really wish you hadn't done that." Chrissy heard the note of panic in Caroline's voice.

"Cara, I'm telling you, you and Bart were made for each other. Besides, I told him that you would love to meet him." Madeleine frowned. "Honestly, Cara, now if you don't go out with him, I'll look like a complete fool! You will go out with him, won't you?" Madeleine pressed.

Caroline shifted uncomfortably. "Okay, I'll go out with him once, but I can't promise you anything beyond that."

Madeleine grinned. "You don't have to promise me anything beyond that. I have a feeling that one date with Bart Reed is all it's going to take, and you both will be head over heels in love." She looked at the watch on her thin wrist and gasped. "Oh, I've got to run. Cara, once you meet Bart, you'll be thanking me. I just know it." She jumped up and gave the two cousins an airy wave, then disappeared out the door of the ice-cream parlor.

"I guess you aren't exactly thrilled by your prospective date," Chrissy observed, tipping up the plastic ice-cream container in an effort to get every last drop of the gooey remains.

"You guess right," Caroline replied with a heavy sigh. "The only guy I want to go out with is Luke. And a blind date—that's the worst." Caroline's face expressed her feeling of dread.

Chrissy grinned broadly. "I wouldn't know anything about blind dates. Back in Danbury, everyone knows everyone else, so it's impossible to have a blind date."

"Well, take my word for it, blind dates are horrid." She looked at Chrissy miserably, pushing away her dish of half-eaten ice cream. "Oh, Chrissy, you know how hard it is for me to meet new people, and the thought of spending an entire evening with a boy I don't even know makes me feel sick to my stomach."

"Sounds like fun to me," Chrissy replied lightly. "It's always fun to meet new people and find out all about them."

Caroline shook her head impatiently. "It's easy for you, Chrissy. You always find it so easy to make new friends. And you don't think anything of striking up a conversation with anyone who happens to be nearby. It's just not that simple for me."

Chrissy smiled sympathetically, knowing that

her cousin was right. "Why didn't you just tell Maddie no?"

"I couldn't just tell her no," Caroline replied in a small voice. "I couldn't let her down like that. You heard her, she'll look like a fool if I don't go."

"Cara, why do you always do this?" Chrissy eyed her cousin firmly. "You're always doing things that you don't really want to do just to make other people happy."

"I do not," Caroline protested.

"Yes, you do. Cara, how long did you continue taking dancing lessons when you didn't really want to, just to make your mother happy?" Chrissy asked. "How many different committees have you been on just because you didn't want anyone to be mad at you?"

"Okay, okay, I get your point," Caroline replied glumly. "But that still doesn't help me now. I guess I'm stuck going out with this Bart once."

"It's just one night, one date," Chrissy offered.

"Yeah, right." Caroline obviously wasn't encouraged.

"Cara, I was wondering something," Chrissy began thoughtfully.

"About that club that Madeleine mentioned, that Pine Hills Country Club . . ."

"What about it?"

"Well, it sounds like something I might be interested in. I mean, she said it was a country club, and I'm from the country . . . ." She stopped as Caroline let out a burst of laughter. "What's so funny?" Chrissy demanded.

"Oh, Chrissy," Caroline tried to swallow her laughter. "There are times when you are priceless!" She stood up, giggling once again. "Come on, let's go home."

Chrissy followed her cousin to the street outside Mama's, a big smile on her face. *For Pete's sake, of course I know a country club isn't for farmers,* she thought. *But I cheered up Cara, and that's what counts.*

Chapter 3

After leaving the ice-cream parlor, the girls trudged up the hill toward home. Chrissy, sensing that Caroline had once again fallen into a miserable silence, tried to contain her naturally bubbly nature. She wished there was something she could do to help her cousin. She hated to see anyone sad or upset, especially Caroline. *She takes everything so seriously,* Chrissy thought to herself as the girls climbed the stairs to the Kirby apartment. *Why can't she just think of her blind date as a sort of adventure? That's what I would do if I were in her place.*

Once at home, the cousins went to their bedroom, each girl flopping on her own bed. Lately it had become a habit for them to tackle their homework right after school, leaving their evenings free for more enjoyable activities.

The bedroom was quiet as each girl concentrated on homework. The silence was broken only by the occasional rustling of textbook pages being turned and Chrissy's grunts of dissatisfaction as she tried to write a short story—her senior literature homework assignment.

"Rats, rats, double rats!" Chrissy hissed as she managed to erase not only the mistake on her paper, but the paper itself as well. She glared at the hole in her paper, then looked up at Caroline as her cousin uttered a deep sigh of misery.

Caroline lay on her back, and instead of doing homework she was once again reading the latest letter she had received from Luke. Unconsciously, she sighed again, the sigh sounding so unhappy that Chrissy felt a tug of sympathy touch her heart. She could easily remember the pangs of loneliness that had hit her each time she had received a letter from Ben. Ben was behind her now. *But I still remember how hard it is to be so far away from the boy you love,* she thought. "You've really got it bad, haven't you Cara?" she said softly.

Caroline looked up from the letter in surprise. "Oh, I'm sorry. Was I bothering you?"

"Nah." Chrissy grinned. "Remember, I grew up on a farm. I'm used to listening to lovesick cows." Her teasing smile softened, but Caroline didn't respond, just sighed once again.

"You really hate the idea of this blind date Friday night, don't you?" Chrissy observed.

Caroline nodded and tucked a strand of her hair behind her ear. "It's really dumb, isn't it." She smiled wistfully. "I know Luke and I decided we could date other people." She looked at Chrissy, her blue eyes darkened with misery. "But, I just don't really feel like dating anyone right now, especially somebody I have never met before."

"But, Cara, Madeleine was right. It sounds like you and this Bart guy would be perfect for each other," Chrissy said.

"I will admit, from what Maddie said, it sounds like Bart Reed and I would have a lot in common," Caroline said, sighing in frustration. "But François and I had a lot in common and we didn't exactly click." A soft, dreamy expression stole over Caroline's features. "But Luke and I had absolutely nothing in common. A country boy and a city girl—people probably wonder what we see in each other. Yet despite all our differences, there's a special kind of magic between Luke and me." She flushed lightly with embarrassment. "Anyway, having things in common doesn't necessarily make a great relationship. Haven't you ever heard the old saying that opposites attract?" She looked at Chrissy defiantly.

"Hey, I'm on your side!" Chrissy protested. "I just wish there was something I could do to help." She shrugged and turned her attention back to her senior literature assignment, but she could feel her cousin's eyes still on her.

"Chrissy . . ."

Chrissy looked up to see Caroline staring at her with a funny expression on her face. "Do you really mean that? About wishing there was something you could do to help me?" Caroline asked slowly.

"Well sure," Chrissy answered without hesitation.

Caroline looked at her thoughtfully, her blue eyes studying Chrissy.

"Stop looking at me like that." Chrissy giggled nervously, wondering what was going on in her cousin's mind. "You are looking at me like I am some sort of weird biology experiment."

Caroline grinned and sat up on the bed, looking at Chrissy sharply. "Yes . . . eyes, I think it would work . . ." she said aloud to herself.

"*Mama mia*, Cara, are you trying to drive me crazy?" Chrissy also sat up and faced her cousin. "What on earth are you talking about?"

"Trading places," Caroline replied simply.

Chrissy looked at her in confusion. "Trading places? What do you mean?"

"You could go out with Bart on Friday night and pretend to be me!" Caroline eyed Chrissy eagerly.

"Caroline Kirby, that is the nuttiest idea I have ever heard!" Chrissy stared at her cousin in shock, but her blue eyes began to twinkle with a devilish gleam. What surprised her most wasn't the notion of trading places, but that Caroline had thought of such a crazy plan.

"Think about it," Caroline continued. "You would only have to carry it off for one night. We both have blond hair and blue eyes, and people are always telling us how much we look alike. If Maddie told Bart Reed what I look like, she would have been describing you, too!" She looked at Chrissy pleadingly. "I really don't want to go, Chrissy. Would you do it for me, please?"

Chrissy grinned good-naturedly. "Cara, you know I would be happy to do anything in the world for you. After all, what are cousins for?" She giggled at Caroline's look of relief. "Besides," she teased, "Madeleine did mention something about Bart Reed being devastatingly handsome!"

"Ha! So much for the loving cousin routine." Caroline laughed, throwing a bed pillow at Chrissy's head.

Chrissy easily ducked the pillow and stood up, grinning at her cousin teasingly. "I suppose this means that on Friday night I will have to act really serious and shy like you."

"You make me sound like a real bore," Caroline said in a small voice.

"Ah, Cara, you aren't a bore." Chrissy instantly regretted her teasing, knowing how insecure her cousin could be at times. "You are smart and thoughtful and sweet, and the very best cousin I could ever have." Chrissy gave her cousin a big hug. "I only hope I can carry off acting like you for a whole night. After all, if I do something dumb, Bart will think you did it."

Caroline looked at her with a stricken expression. "Oh, I never thought about that."

"Don't worry," Chrissy laughed assuringly. "I promise you I won't say holy mazoly or holy cow one single time the whole night."

Caroline grinned weakly. "Somehow that doesn't make me feel any better."

"Relax, I'll be great. I'll be soft-spoken and sophisticated, and I'll talk about all my experiences as a ballerina." Chrissy leapt off Caroline's bed. Standing on her toes with her arms forming a circle above her head, she struck a comical ballet pose. "I will dance the dance of the dead swan from *Swan Lake* for dear old Bart." She gave a loud squawk and began to waddle around on the bedroom floor.

"That looks more like the dance of the dead duck!" Caroline giggled, her giggles changing to uproarious laughter as Chrissy attempted a ballet turn, tangling up her feet and falling smack on her bottom with a tremendous thud that shook the walls.

Almost immediately, Mrs. Langdon from the apartment below began pounding on the ceiling in protest of Chrissy's noisy performance. The two cousins looked at each other guiltily, then burst out into laughter.

That evening, Caroline and Chrissy sat with Caroline's parents in the Kirby living room. Caroline's mother and father sat in large armchairs opposite each other, and the two girls sat on the sofa. Chrissy and Caroline pretended to watch the television news, but every few seconds one or the other would glance at the telephone or at the hands on the clock approaching seven o'clock, then stifle a small giggle.

At the commercial, Richard Kirby eyed the two girls with amusement. "I have never known the newscast to be quite so funny," he observed.

"Oh, it's not the news," Chrissy explained hastily, then looked at Caroline for help.

"It's just a little something Chrissy and I are planning," Caroline grinned mischievously at her parents.

"With you two, a little something means trouble," Mrs. Kirby remarked, shaking her head in amusement.

Just then, the telephone rang. Chrissy and Caroline looked at each other and giggled with excitement. Before either girl could answer the phone, Mr. Kirby picked it up.

"Yes . . . eyes, just a minute." He held out the receiver toward Caroline. "Cara, honey, it's for you."

Caroline gave Chrissy a nod, and with another small giggle, Chrissy jumped up. "I'll take that." She grinned at her uncle and took the phone from him.

For a moment she stood very still, taking several deep breaths as she clutched the receiver. *Now remember, you're not Chrissy Madden anymore, you're Caroline Kirby,* she reminded herself. Taking a final, deep breath, Chrissy uttered a soft hello into the phone.

"Is this Caroline?" asked a deep, rich voice.

"Yes, this is Cara," Chrissy tried to ignore Cara's barely suppressed giggles and her Uncle Richard and Aunt Edith's looks of curiosity.

"Cara, my name is Bart Reed. I'm a friend of Madeleine Walsh." He paused a moment, then continued. "I realize blind dates are rather old-fashioned, but after Madeleine told me all about you, I couldn't help but be intrigued. It seems we have a lot in common."

For a moment Chrissy was mesmerized by the voice on the other end of the line, then she realized that Bart had stopped talking and was waiting for her to say something.

"Oh, yes, Maddie told me all about you, too." Chrissy turned around so that her back was to Caroline, knowing that if she saw her cousin's laughing face she would burst into more uncontrollable giggles of her own.

"The San Francisco Ballet Company is presenting *Coppelia* on Friday night, and I was wondering if perhaps you'd like to go with me."

"That sounds marvelous," Chrissy answered in her most sophisticated voice, covering up the fact that she'd never heard of *Coppelia*.

"Good, I'll pick you up about seven o'clock on Friday evening, if that's okay."

"Of course," Chrissy replied smoothly, and gave Bart the Kirby's address.

"I am really looking forward to meeting you," Bart told her. "See you on Friday."

Chrissy slowly hung up the receiver and turned

around to face Caroline. "Whoopee!" She burst out excitedly. "He bought it, Cara. He really bought it!"

"Would you two care to fill us in on what is going on?" Edith Kirby looked at her daughter, then at her niece.

"Cara was fixed up with a blind date for Friday night," Chrissy began, looking at Caroline for help.

"Madeleine Walsh, a friend from the ballet school, fixed it up, and I just couldn't tell her no, but I really don't want to go," Caroline continued.

"And so you have managed to talk Chrissy into going in your place," Mrs. Kirby concluded with a small smile.

"Oh, she didn't have to talk very hard," Chrissy assured her aunt. "I'm always happy to help Cara."

"Yes, especially since Madeleine told us that Bart is devastatingly handsome." Caroline laughed. "Anyway, since Bart doesn't know either of us, Chrissy is going to go out with him on Friday night and pretend that she is me."

Mr. Kirby grinned. "Sounds like devious feminine wiles to me. I'm glad I'm not this boy. He probably has no idea what he's let himself in for."

"And with a little luck, he'll never know," Chrissy remarked over her shoulder as she followed her cousin down the hall to their bedroom.

"So, where is he taking you on Friday night?" Caroline asked.

Chrissy flopped down on her bed, as Caroline

paced the floor in front of her as if she was a lawyer cross-examining a witness. "He said we were going to see the San Francisco Ballet Company do something called *Coppelia*. Apparently, Madeleine told him all about my ballet training, so he thought I would enjoy it." Chrissy paused as a strange look crossed Caroline's face. "Cara," she reached out to touch her cousin's shoulder. "It isn't too late for you to change your mind and go with Bart." She smiled at her cousin in gentle understanding. "I know how much you love the ballet."

"I do love the ballet," Caroline's voice was wistful, then she shook her head and smiled at Chrissy firmly. "But I put all that behind me when I quit Madame's class." She grinned at Chrissy. "As far as I'm concerned, Bart Reed is all yours!"

"As long as I pretend to be you," Chrissy reminded her with a giggle.

But Caroline's face was serious again. "We can't let anyone know what we are planning," she warned her cousin. "We can't even tell any of our friends about it. We can't take any chances. I wouldn't want Madeleine to find out; she would be mad at me forever!"

Chrissy giggled. "I feel like we are planning some sort of secret mission. Operation: Blind Date. This date will self-destruct at the stroke of midnight on Friday."

Caroline smiled. "We'll just tell all our friends that I have a date for Friday night and you are planning on closeting yourself all evening to catch up on some studying."

"And if I happen to see anyone we know at the ballet, I'll just hide behind the seats in front of us," Chrissy replied confidently. But inside, her stomach flipped over. Could she really trick Bart into believing she was Caroline?

Chapter 4

Chrissy took her mission very seriously. All that week she kept Caroline awake at night asking questions about her cousin's life. She wanted to make sure to get every detail right if Bart should ask any questions.

"Cara, tell me again about all the places you have visited overseas," Chrissy whispered across the darkened bedroom. She could just see her cousin's silhouette in the sliver of light seeping in beneath the window curtain. It was Wednesday night and the two girls had only gone to bed moments earlier.

Caroline sighed tiredly. She had been exhausted all day because Chrissy had kept her up half the previous night talking about her childhood. Still, she was grateful that Chrissy had

agreed to go on the date, and with such dedica-
tion, their plan couldn't fail.

"Well, I've been to France a couple of times,
mostly in Paris," she answered, her voice floating
across the darkness of the bedroom.

"Tell me about Paris," Chrissy prompted.

Caroline's bedsprings squeaked loudly as she
turned over and faced Chrissy. A distant foghorn
sounded from the bay below.

"Paris is beautiful. There are so many things to
see there. The Eiffel Tower, Nôtre Dame
Cathedral, the Louvre, the Arc de Triomphe . . ."

Chrissy rolled over on her back and stared up
at the darkness of the bedroom ceiling, trying to
imagine what it would be like to go to all the
exciting places that Caroline had visited. *I
wonder if she realizes how lucky she is,* Chrissy
thought.

". . . and on the Left Bank there are lots of art-
ists and musicians, and—"

"Hold it, hold it," Chrissy laughed. "I just
wanted to get a general idea in case Bart has
been to France and mentions something about
it." Chrissy shifted restlessly on the bed, too
keyed up with the prospect of the evening with
Bart to be able to sleep. "Where else have you
been? Didn't you mention something about being
in London?"

"Oh, Chrissy, London is absolutely brilliant!"
Caroline enthused. "Of all the places I have been,
London is one of my very favorites. There is so

much pomp and circumstance, so many wonderful traditions and customs."

"I thought pomp and circumstance was a song," Chrissy cut in. "You know, that thing they always play at graduations. Dum-dum- de-dum-dum . . ."

Caroline giggled and clapped her hands over her ears in mock horror at the sound of Chrissy's horrendous, off-key humming. "I'm not talking about that kind of pomp and circumstance. I mean all the formal ceremonies, like the changing of the guard in front of Buckingham Palace, and the presenting of the key at the Tower of London."

Chrissy tried to imagine the things that Caroline described, but her mind drew a blank. "Holy cow, I'll never be able to pull this off," she wailed. "Buckingham Palace and the Arc de Triomphe . . . I don't know anything about any of those places." She flopped back on her back. "Why couldn't the most exciting place you've ever visited have been Des Moines, Iowa? Now that I could have talked about!"

Caroline giggled. "Chrissy, it really isn't important that you know every single detail about all the places I've been. If Bart wanted to know about places overseas, he would have made a date with a travel agent." Caroline smiled at her cousin. "All you have to do is be yourself."

Chrissy rolled her eyes. "Don't you mean that all I have to do is be you?"

"Oh yeah," Caroline giggled again. "I almost forgot for a minute." She looked at Chrissy threateningly in the dim light. "Don't you make the same mistake! When you are out with Bart, you can't forget for one single second that you are supposed to be me!"

"Don't worry," Chrissy said firmly. "I will be so perfect that dear Bart will think himself madly in love with Cara Kirby!"

"I don't want him to fall madly in love with me," Caroline yawned sleepily. "I just want you to get through the date with him on Friday night, then I'll tell Madeleine I thought he was very nice, but I don't intend to see him again." She closed her eyes, giving a sleepy yawn. "Good night Chrissy."

"Good night Cara." Chrissy turned over on her stomach and hugged her pillow to her chest. Although she was still nervous, she was looking forward to her date with Bart. There was something very exciting about the thought of spending an entire evening pretending to be somebody else. *A real adventure,* she thought to herself, *a true challenge. Besides,* she decided with a sudden pang of loneliness, *it would be nice to have a boyfriend again. Cara is so wrapped up in Luke, it makes me realize what I'm missing. Well, at least I've got a date for Friday, thanks to Cara. Wouldn't it be wonderful . . .*

She hugged her pillow tighter and tried to imagine what Bart would be like. She knew already that he had a wonderful voice, and Madeleine had said he was really handsome. She hoped Bart Reed didn't turn out to be a boring snob. Caroline had told her that the Forsythe School was one of the most exclusive private boys' schools in the United States. Oh well, she closed her eyes sleepily. Like she had said, it was just one night, one date, certainly no big deal!

The following night, Caroline had just dozed off when she was awakened by Chrissy, calling her from across the bedroom.

"Cara . . . Cara, are you awake?" Chrissy whispered loudly.

"No," Caroline said sleepily.

"Oh . . . sorry," Chrissy said in a small voice. "Go back to sleep and I won't bother you anymore." She paused a moment. "Really, I just had a teeny-weeny, little question to ask you, but it can wait until morning."

"What?" Caroline asked irritably, knowing she would never get to sleep until Chrissy had her question answered.

"Never mind," Chrissy answered faintly. "It can wait until morning."

"Chrissy, I am awake now, so you'd better ask me that question," Caroline snapped.

"Well, I was just thinking," Chrissy began eagerly, "if I'm going to the ballet tomorrow night and if I am supposed to act like you, then wouldn't it help if I knew something about this *Coppelia* thing?"

Caroline sighed reluctantly. Chrissy did have a point. "*Coppelia* is the name of a ballet also known as *The Girl With the Enamel Eyes*," Caroline began. "The basic story of *Coppelia* is that there is a toy maker named Coppelius who wanted a daughter, and so he makes a lifelike doll to be his daughter."

"Ah, sort of like a dance version of *Pinocchio*," Chrissy said brightly.

Caroline swallowed a groan. How could anyone compare a great ballet to a Disney cartoon? "No, Chrissy, it's not anything like *Pinocchio*," she said patiently. "Anyway, Coppelius names his doll Coppelia and he props her up in a window where the townspeople can see her. Franz, a young townsman falls in love with Coppelia."

"He must have the IQ of a rock to fall in love with a doll," Chrissy giggled.

"Chrissy, stop interrupting or else I am not going to tell you any more," Caroline threatened.

"Sorry," Chrissy apologized softly.

"Anyway, Franz thinks he's in love with Coppelia, which makes his girlfriend, Swanilda, very angry. One evening when Coppelius leaves his shop, he accidently drops the key. Well, Swanilda finds the key, and she and a bunch of her friends sneak into the toy shop. Swanilda wants to confront Coppelia, who she thinks has stolen her boyfriend's love." Caroline closed her eyes, all traces of sleepiness gone as she recalled the story of *Coppelia*. "Once inside the shop, Swanilda and her friends discover all kinds of life-size toys, so they wind them up and dance with them." Caroline smiled softly in the darkness of the bedroom, replaying the ballet in her mind.

"That's my favorite scene—the one where Swanilda and her friends dance with the toys. Then Swanilda discovers Coppelia and realizes that Franz has fallen in love with a doll," Caroline continued. "So Swanilda dresses up like Coppelia, thinking she will teach Franz a lesson." Caroline paused a moment. "Chrissy, are you understanding all this?" She frowned when there was no answer from the opposite bed. "Chrissy?" Still no answer. But through the silence, Caroline could hear the slow regular breathing of her sleeping cousin.

With a small sigh of aggravation, she turned the light off and rolled over, the music of *Coppelia* going around and around in her head.

Chapter 5

"I don't have a thing to wear! Nothing I have is right for tonight!" Chrissy moaned half-hysterically. She was standing in the middle of the bedroom, clad only in her bra and panties, her blond hair neatly twisted around a set of electric curlers. On the floor, on the bed, and draped over the top of the dresser were the entire contents of her side of the girls' closet. For the past forty-five minutes, Chrissy had been frantically trying on clothes, discarding first one, then the next outfit. All her clothes seemed a bit too bold and informal, like Chrissy herself. *And nothing like Caroline,* she thought in despair.

Just then the bedroom door opened.

"Caroline Kirby, where on earth have you been?" Chrissy demanded.

"I went out for some ice cream with Tracy." Caroline looked around the room. "Am I right to guess that you don't know what to wear for tonight, or have you suddenly decided to do some spring cleaning in your closet?" she asked dryly.

"Cara, you've got to help me find something." She looked at her cousin frantically. "What would you wear for an evening at the ballet with a boy like Bart Reed?"

Caroline walked over to the closet and studied her wardrobe for a moment. "I would probably wear something like this." She took a white, pleated skirt from the closet, and handed the skirt to Chrissy to hold. "And for the top . . ." she pulled out a pale peach-colored silky blouse and a long blue sweater with a lacy white collar. She held them both out before her. "I'd wear one of these—probably the blue sweater. It would bring out the beautiful blue of my eyes," she said jokingly as she batted her eyelashes.

Chrissy grabbed the blue sweater out of her cousin's hand. "If it's good enough for your blue eyes, it's good enough for my blue eyes." She paused a moment and looked at Caroline hesitantly. "Can I borrow them?"

"Of course," Caroline smiled. "After all, it's in my best interest for you to look really good tonight. I wouldn't want Bart to tell everyone that Cara Kirby doesn't know how to dress properly."

"Oh, Cara." Chrissy lay the skirt and sweater carefully on her bed, then turned back to face her cousin. "All week this has seemed like such fun, thinking about pretending to be you for a night. But, now that the time is finally here, I have to admit I'm sort of nervous."

"Don't worry," Caroline assured her. "It really isn't so hard to be me. All you really have to remember is that I'm usually pretty shy and quiet around boys."

"If I really did something to mess up this evening, it wouldn't exactly be the end of the world, would it?" Chrissy looked at Caroline anxiously.

"No. I probably just wouldn't talk to you anymore." She laughed at Chrissy's look of horror. "Don't worry, you'll be fine, but I suggest you get into these clothes quickly because Bart should be here in around twenty minutes."

"Twenty minutes!" Chrissy screeched. She yanked the curlers out of her hair with one hand while unzipping the skirt with the other.

Exactly fifteen minutes later, Chrissy stood before her cousin, awaiting final approval. As Caroline inspected the new Chrissy, a pleased smile crossed her face. The blue sweater fell to just below Chrissy's hips, and indeed it did bring out the vivid blue color of her eyes. The lacy white collar made the sweater look very elegant, and complemented the white skirt. Chrissy's hair was a sleek, shiny mass lightly curling on her shoulders, and the light touch of makeup enhanced her pretty features.

"Perfect," Caroline announced. "Simple, yet

elegant, fashionable, and sophisticated." She frowned a moment. "There is only one thing missing . . ." She ran to her dresser and rummaged around in one of the drawers. "Here it is!" She withdrew a black velvet jeweler's box and handed it to Chrissy.

Chrissy opened the box, gasping at the sight of the lustrous string of pearls and matching pearl earrings. "Oh Cara . . . I couldn't," she protested.

"Yes you can, and you will," Caroline said smoothly. She took the string of pearls from Chrissy, and twirling her cousin around, fastened them around her slender neck. "Now, put on the earrings."

Chrissy did as she was instructed, then looked at Caroline expectantly. "Now you look perfect, absolutely perfect." Caroline grinned. "You look just like me when I go out to the ballet." Caroline clapped her hands together in excitement. "It's too bad Mom and Dad are already out for the evening. I wish they could see—" Caroline stopped in midsentence as the doorbell sounded.

"That must be him," Chrissy whispered, her heart pounding with anticipation.

"Well, you'd better not keep him waiting," Caroline said.

Chrissy just stared at her cousin. "But aren't you going to come meet him?" she asked. Suddenly her nerves got the better of her and she didn't want to face Caroline's blind date all on her own.

"I can't meet him, Chrissy. In fact, just to be on

the safe side, I'm not even going to peek down the hall. Now hurry up," Caroline scolded as the doorbell rang again.

Chrissy gave her cousin a nervous grin. "Well, Chrissy, have fun studying tonight."

Caroline giggled. "And you enjoy your evening with Bart, Cara." For a moment the two cousins stood grinning at each other, their blue eyes sparkling merrily, then Chrissy went out to meet her date.

As she opened the door, the first thing she noticed was Bart's pink sweater. It took a special boy to look good in a pastel-pink sweater, and Bart was definitely special. He looked gorgeous. The pink sweater hugged his broad shoulders, and a pair of tailored, gray slacks covered his long legs. His dark brown hair fell neatly into place, and his brown eyes were warm and friendly. *Holy Mazoly! Madeleine was right,* Chrissy thought. *He's the most devastatingly handsome boy I've ever seen!*

"Cara . . . Cara Kirby?" He asked hesitantly.

"Yes," Chrissy flushed, realizing she had been staring at him. "Yes, I'm Cara, and you must be Bart Reed."

He nodded with a friendly smile. "Are you all ready to go?" She nodded and stepped out of the Kirby apartment. Together they walked down the stairs and into the pleasant, chilly night air.

"So, Madeleine told me you are quite a dancer," Bart said once they were sitting in his sports car and on their way to the Civic Center.

"Oh yes, I started taking ballet lessons when I was about six years old," Chrissy answered easily.

"Then you should really enjoy this production of *Coppelia* this evening," Bart said.

"*Coppelia . . . The Girl With the Enamel Eyes,*" Chrissy said, pleased that Cara's tutoring of the night before was already paying off.

He grinned at her. "You sure know your ballet. Tell me more about your lessons. Maddie told me that you used to be in her class," he prompted.

"Oh, I wouldn't want to bore you." Chrissy smiled nervously.

"Please, you really won't bore me. Actually, I'm fascinated by ballet. I think it's amazing how you dancers can do such difficult moves and make them look completely natural." He laughed softly, a low, pleasant sound that sent shivers up and down Chrissy's arms. "My mother is a big fan of ballet, so I guess it has rubbed off on me."

For the first time in her life, Chrissy wished she really was a ballet dancer. *But he doesn't know that I'm not a dancer,* she consoled herself. *He thinks I am Cara.* She fell silent as Bart maneuvered his car into a parking space at the Civic Center.

"Thank you," she murmured politely as he opened her car door and helped her out. She was amazed at how weak-kneed she felt when he took hold of her elbow and smiled down at her. He had such a handsome smile. She could smell the pleasant scent of his cologne, a spicy, tangy scent, and suddenly she was glad that Caroline hadn't wanted to come tonight. *Thanks for letting me go on your blind date, Cara,* Chrissy said silently. *I think this is the best idea you've ever had!*

Chrissy had never been to a ballet before, although Caroline had managed to drag her to the Civic Center for an opera one evening. While she hadn't understood much of the opera, Chrissy had been fascinated by the plush theater, the extravagant chandeliers, and the audience in their furs and jewels. Tonight the Civic Center was as elegant as she remembered it, but this time Chrissy tried to act as sophisticated as the people around her.

"*Coppelia* is one of my favorite ballets, although my first choice would probably be *Giselle,*" Bart commented as they took their seats in the front row of the balcony.

"Yes, I think *Giselle* is a beautiful ballet," she answered, having absolutely no idea what *Giselle* was about.

He looked at her in surprise. "Most people describe *Giselle* as tragic," he said.

"Beautifully tragic, that's what I meant," Chrissy said hurriedly, relieved as the houselights dimmed and the conductor appeared.

As the curtain rose and the ballet began to unfold, Chrissy was grateful that she had heard part of the story from Cara. Knowing a little bit of the plot helped her follow the action taking place on the stage below. As she gazed at the beautiful costumes and watched the dancers twirling and leaping, she suddenly understood Caroline's long-standing fascination with the ballet. It was all so beautiful. Oh, to be able to move like the dancers on the stage, she thought wistfully. It would be wonderful to be so graceful, to be able to defy gravity and leap so high in the air.

By the time the intermission came, Chrissy was on the very edge of her seat, her elbows perched on the balcony, totally enthralled by the beauty of the ballet. When the houselights came on for the brief intermission, Chrissy blinked, dazed for a moment, then she quickly slid back in her seat and smiled at Bart self-consciously.

"Sorry." She blushed, embarrassed that Bart had caught her slipping out of character. *Cara would never hang over the balcony like that,* she scolded herself. *I've got to be more careful.*

"Don't apologize." Bart smiled at her, his brown eyes sparkling warmly. "It's nearly as interesting to watch your excitement as it is to watch the ballet."

"I guess I just have trouble hiding my feelings about ballet," Chrissy answered, thinking she sounded very Caroline-like.

"There's nothing wrong with that," Bart said. "In fact, it's rather nice to be with somebody who isn't afraid to show her feelings." He gazed at her seriously. "There are times when I get tired of being around people who always try so hard to appear bored."

"Well, I'm certainly not bored tonight. I feel like

I'm seeing my very first ballet," Chrissy declared, giving Bart a smile. *Holy cow! Have I ever hit the jackpot,* she thought. *Not only does Bart Reed look like a model, he also seems really nice.*

As the second half of the ballet began, Bart's hand found Chrissy's, enclosing around it in a warm grasp. *I wonder if he can hear my heartbeat,* she thought. The feel of his hand over hers and the scent of his after-shave in the air, made Chrissy's heart beat a rapid tattoo in her chest.

The rest of the ballet passed with Chrissy concentrating more on the boy next to her than on the ballet onstage. In the semidarkness, she shot him furtive glances, entranced by the combination of strength and tenderness apparent in his face. His eyes were such a warm shade of brown, with tiny lines that radiated out from the corners as if he made a habit of smiling. His nose was straight, and his smile revealed a set of even white teeth. He was easily the best-looking boy she had ever been out with. And on top of that, he was genuinely friendly, and not snobby at all. But the very best part was that he seemed to like her. *Don't get too confident,* she warned herself. *It's not you he likes, it's your imitation of Cara that he likes—quiet, sensitive Caroline Kirby the ballet dancer.* Chrissy glanced at him again and smiled to herself. *But for tonight, I am Cara,* she thought happily, *and as long as I can keep on acting like Cara, everything will be just fine!*

"How about some coffee," Bart suggested as they walked back to his car after the ballet. "I know a wonderful little place where we can get a great cup of cappuccino or espresso, and it's quiet enough that we can talk and really get to know each other better." He smiled at her and Chrissy felt her heart begin its rapid thudding again.

"That sounds fine." She smiled at him faintly. At least going out for a cup of coffee was harmless. All she had to worry about was the part where they talked and got to know each other better. *Mama mia*, Chrissy thought, *I just hope I can carry this off!*

Chapter 6

The Italian Bistro was a charming, little coffee shop with large green plants hanging down from the low ceiling and cheerful red-checked cloths on each table. Muted lights and flickering candles set a romantic mood.

"I come here pretty often," Bart explained to Chrissy as the hostess led them to a table in the back. "This place always reminds me of my trip to Italy. My parents and I traveled to Rome the summer I was ten years old." He paused, and as he looked at Chrissy, she noticed his dark eyes shimmer in the golden light of the candles. "It's funny, Rome is supposed to be one of the most beautiful cities in the world, yet all I can remember are all the little bistros and sidewalk cafes." He leaned forward in his chair.

"Madeleine mentioned to me that you have done quite a bit of traveling."

Chrissy shrugged nonchalantly. "I've been to London a few times, and France ... mostly Paris."

Bart's eyes lit up brightly. "I love Paris. Out of all the places I have been, I think Paris is one of my favorites." He leaned back in his chair. "Tell me, what did you enjoy most about Paris?"

For a moment, a wave of helpless panic swept over Chrissy. She tried to remember something—anything—that Caroline had told her about Paris, but her mind was blank. As Bart looked at her expectantly, Chrissy grasped at the only French thing that popped into her mind.

"Croissants ... I loved the croissants." She looked at him in horror. How stupid could she be? Croissants ... for crying out loud!

Bart looked at her for a long moment, then threw back his head and laughed. "Oh, Cara, we really make a terrific pair of world-weary travelers. All I can remember about Rome is the bistros, and all you can remember about Paris is the croissants!" He reached across the table and gently took her hand in his. "We make quite a pair, Caroline Kirby." His warm gaze lingered on her face.

Chrissy looked at him with an enormous sense of relief. *Thank goodness I didn't blow it,* she thought, *but if he doesn't stop looking at me like that I am going to melt into a puddle beneath the table.*

At that moment, the waiter approached their table with a friendly smile. "Are you ready to order?"

"What would you like, Cara?" Bart asked, removing his hand from hers.

Chrissy looked at him dumbly. She hadn't had a chance to glance through the menu yet. She wondered what Cara would do in this situation. "What are you having?" she asked Bart hesitantly.

"I think I'll have a cup of espresso," Bart replied.

"I'll have the same," Chrissy said with a bright smile. *There, that wasn't so difficult,* she told herself. *Espresso—it must be express coffee. Does that mean Bart is in a hurry?* she wondered with a sinking feeling.

"Now, tell me about your ballet," Bart said once the waiter had departed with their order. "Madeleine mentioned to me that at one time you had considered becoming a professional dancer, but then you quit."

Chrissy nodded. "I quit last year."

"What made you decide to give it up?" Bart looked at her curiously.

Chrissy paused a moment, thinking about all the reasons why Caroline had decided to give up her rigorous ballet training the year before. "I was working very hard at my ballet, going to lessons every night and sacrificing everything else that was important. One day I nearly fainted because I hadn't eaten enough, and I didn't have any time to spend with my friends." Chrissy's face was serious as she remembered the pain Caroline had gone through in making her decision to quit ballet. "Ballet stopped being fun and I realized the only reason I was working so hard at it was to please my parents and the teacher." She smiled at him. "Now that I've decided I don't want to be a professional ballerina, I don't feel all that pressure, and I love ballet again."

"Madeleine told me you are very talented," Bart said.

Chrissy grinned. "Maddie does tend to exaggerate."

"I think you're being modest," Bart replied, a warm smile on his handsome features. "Personally, I have two left feet and a horrible sense of rhythm." His smile softened. "I would love to see you dance some time. I can just imagine you twirling gracefully across the room."

Chrissy swallowed a desire to laugh. Oh, if only he had seen her the other day, gracefully leaving the bedroom with a pair of dirty jeans dangling from her big toe. She looked down at the table, not knowing what to say and hoping he would interpret her silence as more modesty.

She looked up with relief as the waiter arrived at their table. "Oh, what cute little cups," Chrissy exclaimed in delight as the waiter set a tiny cup and saucer in front of each of them. The little cups and saucers reminded her of the miniature tea set her great aunt had given her for Christmas one year.

"But espresso coffee is always served in demi-tasse cups," Bart said, a puzzled look on his face.

"Oh ... I knew that," Chrissy's face flushed hotly. "Uh ... I was talking about the cute designs, all these pretty little flowers," she stammered, trying to cover up her mistake.

"I guess they are kind of pretty," Bart replied.

Stupid, stupid, stupid! Chrissy thought to herself angrily. *Cara would never have made such a stupid mistake. She would have known that espresso was served in baby cups called demi-whatevers.* Too embarrassed to look at him, Chrissy picked up the small cup and took a big gulp. As the hot, bitter liquid slid down her throat, her eyes flew wide open and she fought to control a shudder of revulsion. It was the most horrid stuff she had ever tasted! She looked up and forced a small smile at Bart, as if she thought the espresso was delicious.

Bart stared at Chrissy in amazement. "I've never met anyone who could drink espresso coffee black." He pulled the sugar bowl toward his cup. "Everyone I know adds sugar and lemon peel to their espresso." She watched as he added two heaping teaspoons of sugar, then plopped a sliver of lemon into his small cup.

Chrissy smiled at him in what she hoped looked like confidence. "I got used to drinking it black when I was training seriously in ballet. All of that sugar isn't good for a dancer's system."

"I never thought of that." Bart looked at her

with admiration. "I guess there were lots of things you had to learn to do without."

Chrissy nodded with a silent sigh of relief. *This is much harder than I thought it would be,* she decided. *I thought that all I'd have to do was control my big mouth, but I must admit there's a lot more to Caroline behind her shyness. She always knows what to do no matter what the situation. If I live in San Francisco for the rest of my life, I will probably still do stupid things.* She peered into the little coffee cup before her. She still had a half a cup of the vile liquid, and she didn't dare ask for sugar and lemon peel now. *Oh, Chrissy Madden, you get yourself into the most darned-awful messes,* she thought, smiling at Bart as if nothing was wrong.

"You have suddenly gotten very quiet," Bart observed. "What are you thinking about?"

"I was just thinking about my cousin," Chrissy replied truthfully.

"Your cousin?" Bart's forehead wrinkled in curiosity. "Does your cousin live here in San Francisco?"

Chrissy nodded. "As a matter of fact, she's been living with my family for the last year and a half. She comes from a farm in Iowa."

"A farm in Iowa," Bart repeated, as if he wasn't sure he'd heard correctly. "I can't imagine what you would have in common with a farm girl from Iowa."

"Oh, you'd be surprised," Chrissy swallowed a giggle, then continued. "Actually, Chrissy is really a lot of fun. She thinks everything about San Francisco is wonderful and exciting." Chrissy's blue eyes twinkled brightly and her face was animated. Now here was a subject she could really talk about! "She doesn't know a lot about big-city ways, but she learns quickly."

"Does she like San Francisco?" Bart asked.

"Oh yes, Chrissy loves it here." Chrissy smiled. It was really fun to talk about herself as if she was somebody else. "The only thing is, there are times when she gets sort of homesick." The smile slowly faded from Chrissy's face as a wave of real homesickness swept over her. She continued talking softly. "Spring is one of the nicest times of year on the farm. Everywhere you look there are signs of new life. The trees bud, the flowers bloom, and everything smells green and fresh." Chrissy shook her head to rid her mind of thoughts of home. "At least that's the way Chrissy describes it," she said self-consciously, realizing she was talking too much. Caroline would never be such a chatterbox.

"It sounds like you and your cousin are very close. She's lucky to have you to show her around the city."

"Yeah, I guess she is," Chrissy said thoughtfully. It was true, she was very lucky to have Caroline. She looked at the flickering candle in the center of their table and suddenly felt depressed. She had only agreed to go on this date with Bart as a favor to Caroline, but now she was dreading the date coming to an end. She looked up at Bart, suddenly wanting to know more about him.

"I've spent almost the entire evening talking about myself," she told him. "Now it's your turn to tell me about you."

Bart shrugged and took a quick sip of his espresso. "There really isn't much to tell," he began thoughtfully. "I'm an only child and I'm a senior at the Forsythe School. I haven't made a final decision on a college yet, but I know that I want to major in journalism." His eyes opened wide, as he leaned forward. "That reminds me, didn't Madeleine tell me that your father is some sort of journalist?"

Chrissy nodded. "Unc . . . Dad writes music reviews for magazines and newspapers."

Bart's face lit up with excitement. "That's the kind of thing that I want to do, but I'd like to cover the whole cultural scene. You know—ballets, art shows, theater—a little of everything." He looked at her curiously. "What about you? Have you decided on college?"

Chrissy shook her head. "I haven't made any final decision, but I am leaning toward Colorado University in Boulder," she answered. *I wish I really were going to Colorado University,* Chrissy thought wistfully. *Cara's so lucky.*

Bart nodded. "That's supposed to be an excellent college." Bart gazed at her thoughtfully, a small smile curving his lips upward. "You know, Madeleine told me you were really nice looking, but there are a lot of things she failed to mention about you."

"Like what?" Chrissy asked faintly. *Uh oh, here it comes,* she thought with a sense of dread. *Somehow she had messed up and he was starting to figure out that she was not Caroline Kirby.* She held her breath as he answered.

"Well, she told me you had blond hair, and blue eyes, but you're still a lot prettier than I expected. In fact, in this candlelight I'd say you look just like an angel." His brown eyes were gazing at her intensely, and Chrissy felt a blush creeping up her neck. "I'm sorry," Bart said immediately. "I didn't mean to embarrass you. I'm just sort of surprised," he continued. "Blind dates really aren't my style and I don't think they're yours either. I'm just really surprised at how much I've enjoyed this evening."

"I've enjoyed it, too," Chrissy replied, returning Bart's gaze.

"And it's so nice to find somebody that I have so much in common with!" He smiled at her softly, then took the last sip of his coffee. "You didn't finish your espresso."

Chrissy grinned. "When you're drinking it black, it doesn't take much to quench your thirst," she explained. Her grin slowly faded and she looked at him reluctantly. "Bart, it's getting pretty late and I really should be getting home." She hated to see the evening end. She had enjoyed pretending to be Caroline, but more than that, she had really enjoyed spending the evening with Bart.

They were both quiet on the ride back to the Kirby apartment. Chrissy wanted to ask him more questions about himself, but somehow she knew that Caroline would never be so inquisitive, so she simply sat quietly. *Oh, I wish this evening would never end,* she thought as Bart reached over and found her hand, grasping it warmly. All too quickly they pulled up outside the Kirbys. Together, with Bart still holding her hand, they slowly climbed the stairs to the apartment.

"Thank you, Bart," she said as they stood before the door. "I really had a good time this evening."

"I enjoyed it, too." Bart said. He glanced down at his feet, then back at Chrissy. "Listen Cara, there's a Shakespeare reading tomorrow night at the park near my house. Do you want to go?"

Chrissy stood very still for a moment. All evening she'd been hoping Bart would ask her out again, but now that he had, she didn't know what to do. She had successfully masqueraded as Caroline once, could she do it again? One look at Bart and her answer became crystal clear. There was no way she would pass up the opportunity to go out with him again.

"I'd love to go," Chrissy answered with a smile.

"Great." He returned the smile, then smoothly gathered her in his arms and brought his lips down to meet hers. His kiss was warm and wonderful, and Chrissy felt a stab of disappointment when he released her. "I'll pick you up at seven tomorrow." He gave her hand a quick squeeze. "Until tomorrow . . ."

"Until tomorrow," Chrissy echoed softly, watching him as he ran lightly down the stairs.

Chapter 7

Quietly Chrissy let herself into the Kirby apartment. *Everyone must be sleeping*, she thought. *I'm so wide awake. I want to sing, and dance, and tell everyone that I just had the most wonderful date of my life.* The natural energy that she had carefully kept suppressed all night was now bubbling over. She could feel the blood racing through her veins, and her heart was beating wildly in her chest.

Settle down, she commanded herself firmly, taking a few deep breaths. *Caroline would not appreciate being awakened in the middle of the night, not even to hear about my—or should I say, her—date. There will be time enough to tell her all about it in the morning*, Chrissy chided herself as she crept down the dark hallway to the girls' bedroom. She stepped out of her shoes and was just about to step out of the white skirt when the bedroom light clicked on.

"So, tell me," Caroline said, sitting up in her bed and facing Chrissy. "Did I have a good time on my date with Bart Reed?"

"Oh, Cara, you had a wonderful time," Chrissy answered, her face lit with a dreamy expression.

"And did Bart have a good time with me?" Caroline asked with a grin.

"Yes, I think so." Chrissy paused a moment and stepped out of the skirt. "He must have had a good time with you because he asked you out again for tomorrow night."

Caroline sat up straighter on her bed and pushed her tousled hair out of her eyes. "He did?" she asked in disbelief. "What are you going to do?"

"What do you think I'm going to do? I'm going to go out with him and pretend to be you again." Chrissy hung up the white skirt, then sat down on the edge of her bed. "Oh, Cara, Bart Reed is like no other boy I have ever gone out with."

"A real babe, huh?" Caroline smiled at her cousin's dreamy expression.

"More than that," Chrissy said thoughtfully. "Madeleine wasn't exaggerating when she said he is devastatingly handsome—he is gorgeous! He has thick, dark brown hair and beautiful brown eyes, and he is tall with wide shoulders. He's so nice, Cara, and very mature." She sighed. "I never dreamed when we were planning our switch that I might really like Bart, and I never expected that he would like me . . . or should I say that he would like you!"

"I am really not a bit surprised that he likes you," Caroline teased. "After all, you were pretending to be me and I *am* pretty wonderful."

Chrissy laughed. "And he especially likes your modesty," she remarked dryly.

"No kidding?"

Chrissy nodded.

"Wow, Chrissy, you must have been really good at being me." Caroline looked at her with grudging admiration.

"Everything went fine until we went to this place called The Italian Bistro and Bart ordered us each a cup of espresso." Chrissy grinned sheepishly. "I didn't know you were supposed to add sugar and a lemon peel, so I just gulped mine down black."

A look of horror crossed Caroline's face. "Oh, Chrissy, that's disgusting!"

"I know," Chrissy agreed. "It reminded me of the time when my brother Tom and I found some chewing tobacco. We each took a big pinch of it and chewed it like bubble gum." Chrissy grimaced at the memory. "We were sick as dogs. I'll never forget the taste of that tobacco juice, and that's exactly how black espresso coffee tastes." She giggled, remembering the expression on Bart's face. "Bart was really shocked. He said he'd never seen anyone drink espresso black."

"What did you say to him?" Caroline asked.

"I told him that sugar isn't good for dancers, so when I was seriously training to be a professional ballerina, I got used to drinking it black."

Caroline laughed. "That was quick thinking," she remarked. Then she asked thoughtfully, "What did you think about *Coppelia?*"

"Oh, Cara, it was really beautiful." Chrissy's face shone with excitement. "I never really understood your fascination with ballet until tonight. The music and the costumes and the dancing all combine to make a sort of magic, don't they?"

Caroline smiled wistfully, and Chrissy knew her cousin was feeling a pang of regret for giving up her dancing lessons. "Yeah, ballet is magical," Caroline replied.

"That reminds me," Chrissy began, a mysterious glint in her eyes. "I have a small little problem to discuss with you."

"What?" Caroline looked at her cousin curiously.

"Bart wants to see me dance some time."

"You mean dance as in ballet dance?" Caroline's voice rose in disbelief, and a wild laugh escaped her lips. "But, you don't know anything about ballet."

"That's sort of what I wanted to talk to you about." Chrissy grinned at her cousin hesitantly.

"Oh no." Caroline flopped back against her pillow. "You aren't serious, are you?"

"If you could just give me a few lessons." Chrissy looked at her cousin pleadingly.

"Chrissy, there is no way that I can teach you in a few lessons what it has taken me over ten years to learn," Caroline began. "Remember when I tried to teach you some steps so you could audition for the school musical last year? Complete disaster!"

"I remember, but this time will be different," Chrissy insisted. She stood up and pulled Caroline's blue sweater over her head, then hung it up.

"Wouldn't it just be easier to tell Bart the truth, tell him that you are not really Cara Kirby?"

"No!" Chrissy said, pulling on her nightgown. She sat on the edge of her bed, an earnest look on her face. "Absolutely not, Cara. It has already gone too far for me to tell Bart that now. I told him all about your life tonight and pretended it was my life. I told him about dancing and traveling." She grinned, her blue eyes sparkling merrily now. "I even told him all about Chrissy, my cousin from Danbury, Iowa!"

"Oh, Chrissy, you didn't!" Caroline giggled.

"I did," Chrissy nodded, but the grin slowly faded from her face. "So you see, I can't tell him that I'm not Caroline Kirby." She smiled dryly. "I guess I'm stuck being you for a little while longer. Do you mind?"

"No, I don't mind," Caroline laughed. "Things were getting sort of boring around here anyway. Besides, this is one mess I feel personally responsible for getting you into."

"So you'll teach me some ballet steps?" Chrissy asked.

"Sure, we can start tomorrow."

"Thanks Cara. You're terrific," Chrissy said, leaping up to give her cousin a quick hug. "And you're also terrific for letting me wear your pearls," she added as she carefully replaced the necklace and earrings in the velvet jeweler's box, then crawled beneath the covers of her bed. "You know, I have to admit, it's harder pretending to be you than I thought it would be."

Caroline yawned sleepily. "I don't know. I think it's pretty easy being me. I'm just waiting for my chance to be you."

Chrissy snorted with laughter. "Cara, you could never pretend to be me. You don't make enough noise." She snorted again at the very thought of her proper cousin trying to act like her.

"Maybe you're right," Caroline said agreeably, leaning over to shut off the bedroom light. "All I know is that right now I'm totally exhausted. Training you to be me is hard work."

"Okay, we can talk more in the morning." Chrissy said, snuggling down in her bed. "Cara . . ." she called to her cousin as a sudden thought struck her. "Do you know anything about Shakespeare?"

"Why?"

"Bart is taking me to a Shakespeare reading in the park tomorrow night and I thought maybe if you knew about Shakespeare, you wouldn't mind . . ."

"No!" Caroline's voice rang out firm and clear across the darkness of the bedroom.

"I haven't even finished my question yet!" Chrissy protested indignantly.

"Chrissy Madden, you don't have to finish the question. It doesn't take a genius to figure out that you are going to ask me if I'll teach you everything there is to know about Shakespeare by tomorrow night."

"Could you?" Chrissy asked in a small voice.

"Absolutely not!" Caroline sighed impatiently. "First of all, it would be completely impossible for me to tell you all about Shakespeare in a single day. Second of all, I refuse to spend my Saturday tutoring you in a subject I don't even like! Besides, I've already agreed to teach you some ballet."

"Okay, Cara, it was just a thought, and thanks in advance for the ballet lessons," Chrissy said in that same small voice.

"Chrissy, I'm really glad you had a good time this evening," Caroline said after a brief silence. "I don't mean to be such a grouch. I guess I'm just a bit jealous that you got to go to the ballet tonight."

Chrissy peered over at her cousin through the darkness. "But Cara, you said you didn't want to go."

"I wanted to go to the ballet, but not with a blind date," Caroline replied. "I really do appreciate you going in my place."

"I should be the one thanking you," Chrissy

said. "When you see how good-looking Bart is, you're going to kick yourself good and hard for handing him over to me."

Caroline laughed confidently. "Not me, for the moment I'm perfectly content as long as I keep getting letters from Luke." Caroline's bedsprings squeaked as she found a more comfortable position. "Good night, Chrissy," she murmured softly.

"'Night, Cara." Chrissy replied, closing her eyes and hugging her pillow tightly as Bart's handsome face loomed in her mind.

Chapter 8

"I will never understand how on earth you can eat all that food so early in the morning," Caroline said as she looked distastefully at Chrissy's plate of pancakes and sausage.

"And I don't know how a growing girl like you can exist all day on a monkey food breakfast." Chrissy grinned, pointing to the banana that Caroline had plucked from the bowl of fresh fruit that sat in the middle of the kitchen table.

Caroline merely smiled and peeled the ripe banana.

"Good morning, girls." Mrs. Kirby came into the kitchen, looking very attractive in a chocolate-brown suit. Rolled up in her hand was the morning newspaper.

"Morning, Aunt Edith," Chrissy smiled brightly.

"Good morning, Mom." Caroline looked at her mother curiously. "Where are you off to so bright and early on a Saturday morning?"

"We're having a showing for a new artist this afternoon at the gallery. I've got to get there early because there are a million details I need to attend to," Mrs. Kirby explained. She put the paper down on the table and poured herself a cup of coffee. After a quick glance at the clock on the oven, she joined the two girls at the kitchen table. "I just have time for a quick cup of coffee and to find out how the date went last night." She looked at Chrissy expectantly.

Chrissy swallowed a bite of pancake and grinned at her aunt. "It was great. I acted just like Caroline. I was as ladylike as I could be. You would have been proud of me, Aunt Edith."

Mrs. Kirby smiled at Chrissy fondly. "Chrissy, I'm very proud of you when you are just being yourself."

Chrissy felt a warm glow at her aunt's words.

"She did such a good job impersonating me that Bart has asked her out again for tonight," Caroline said with a smile.

"Hmmm, sounds serious." Mrs. Kirby's eyes twinkled with amusement as she took a sip of her coffee.

"It must be pretty serious," Caroline replied. "Chrissy has even asked me to teach her some ballet."

Chrissy nodded. "Caroline is going to turn me into a ballet dancer this afternoon, just in case

Bart asks me to do a little pass-de-dew."

Caroline rolled her eyes toward the ceiling. "The term is *pas de deux,*" she said, giving it the proper French pronunciation.

"It sounds like you girls have your work cut out for you. Oh, that reminds me," Aunt Edith began, opening the newspaper. "I noticed Bart's mother's picture in the paper this morning."

"I didn't realize you knew Bart's mother," Caroline said curiously, taking a last bite of her banana and tossing the peel into the garbage can.

"That's a basket. Two points," Chrissy remarked.

"I don't know Mrs. Reed very well. She comes into the gallery occasionally," Aunt Edith said as she thumbed through the pages of the newspaper. "I don't know why I didn't make the connection when you girls were first talking about Bart Reed, but it suddenly struck me yesterday that Bart must be the son that Elizabeth Reed is always talking about. Ah, here it is." She lay the paper flat on the table before the two girls. The cousins' blond heads came together as they both leaned over to see the picture and accompanying article.

"She looks pretty," Caroline observed, looking at the grainy picture of the dark-haired woman.

"Bart looks a lot like his mom," Chrissy said thoughtfully.

"It says here that she was voted chairperson of a committee to raise funds for a new cultural center." Caroline quickly scanned the article.

"Gosh, that sounds pretty important," Chrissy commented, looking at her Aunt curiously. "Is she nice?"

Edith Kirby finished her coffee before answering. "Elizabeth Reed is a well-known patron of the arts in San Francisco." A slightly uncomfortable look crossed Aunt Edith's face. "I really haven't had enough dealings with her to be able to make a personal judgment about her. Besides," she continued with a quick smile to the girls, "does it really matter? After all, you're dating Bart, not his mother!"

"True," Chrissy agreed. "And I probably won't be dating Bart for very long anyway." She looked at her aunt and her cousin with a dry smile. "After all, we all know that I can't keep up this impersonation of Caroline forever!" She grinned. "Holy Mazoly, too much of that and I'll go nuts!"

Caroline and her mother laughed, then Mrs. Kirby looked once again at the clock. "Oops, I've got to run! Your father is going to be at a concert tonight and I'll probably be late at the gallery, so you two girls are on your own this evening."

"No problem," the girls assured her as she waved a quick good-bye and left for her work at the gallery.

"So, other than our ballet lessons, what do you have planned for the day?" Caroline asked Chrissy.

Chrissy took her sticky plate to the sink where she rinsed it and placed it in the dishwasher. "As for what I'm doing today, I don't know. I suppose

I should go to the library and check out some books on Shakespeare." She frowned. "I've heard about his plays, like that Midsummer Nightmare and Much Ado About Something." She paused when she saw the amused expression on her cousin's face, then continued. "In ninth grade we studied about that merchant guy in Italy, but I couldn't understand any of it."

Caroline giggled. "It's *A Midsummer Night's Dream,* and *Much Ado About Nothing,* and that merchant fellow was *The Merchant of Venice.*" She smiled sympathetically. "You really don't need to study up on Shakespeare just for tonight. You're supposed to be me, and I don't know very much about Shakespeare. I've studied some of his plays in school, but I'm certainly not an expert."

"Hey, that's right," Chrissy's face brightened considerably. "If I'm supposed to be you and you don't know much about Shakespeare, then it's okay if I don't know much, either!" She looked at Caroline happily. "Thanks, Cara!"

"Thanks for what?" Caroline asked.

"Thanks for not being an expert on Shakespeare."

Caroline laughed. "You're welcome."

Chrissy heaved a sigh of relief, but then the little line of worry reappeared on her forehead. "Caroline, I know I've been a pain all week, asking you all those questions so I could pretend to be you. And you were so good about helping me decide what to wear last night and even letting me borrow your best clothes and pearls.

And now you've agreed to help me learn some ballet." She looked at her cousin hesitantly. "Would you mind helping me get ready again tonight? I really don't have any idea what to wear to a Shakespeare reading."

"Of course I'll help you," Caroline agreed.

Chrissy threw her arms around her cousin's neck, giving her a happy hug. "Oh, Cara, you are the best, most wonderful cousin in the whole wide world!" she exclaimed.

"You just believe that right now because I can't quote Shakespeare," Caroline laughed. "Now, why don't we get started on those ballet lessons I promised you!"

Fifteen minutes later, the two cousins left their bedrooms, each clad in a pair of Caroline's tights and leotards.

"I've got to start on a diet," Chrissy grumbled, pulling at the uncomfortably tight leotard she wore. "I must be getting fat."

"It's your imagination," Caroline assured her. "Anyway, you're not very good at dieting. You like food too much. Remember when you went on a diet to lose weight for Hunter?"

"How could I forget? I suffered from ice-cream withdrawal symptoms," Chrissy recalled. "And Hunter wasn't even worth it after all that. But Bart—oh, Cara, he's *so* nice!"

Caroline laughed. "Come on, let's teach you some ballet so you can impress him." She tugged on Chrissy's arm, pulling her into the living room where they would have more room for the ballet lesson.

"The first thing you need to learn is the five basic ballet positions," Caroline began. "First, second, third, fourth, and fifth position." As she said them, she demonstrated each one.

"That looks easy enough." Chrissy smiled brightly, then a look of intense concentration crossed her face as she tried to copy Caroline. "First . . . second . . . third . . . fourth . . . fifth . . . ugh!" She groaned loudly as she forced her feet into the unnatural fifth position. "Bart mentioned that ballet requires difficult movements that are unnatural for the human body," she complained. "Now I understand exactly what he was talking about! I feel like a human pretzel!"

Caroline giggled. "It will get easier with practice. Now, let's start working on some pliés."

By the time the girls had been working for two hours, Chrissy was not only completely exhausted, but every muscle in her body was screaming with pain. "I must be doing something wrong," she said, sitting down on the living room floor and pulling off the old pair of ballet shoes Caroline had found for her to wear. "I've got to be doing something wrong to be in all this pain!"

Caroline laughed and executed a flawless ballet turn. "Madame always told us, 'no pain, no gain'!"

"But I'm not sure I want the gain if I have to have all this pain," Chrissy exclaimed, struggling to her feet with another groan. "I'm going to go soak in a long, hot bath," she said, stumbling off to the bathroom still moaning and groaning.

Caroline watched her go, a small smile touching her lips. She knew exactly how Chrissy was feeling, for her own muscles were aching, too. But, to Caroline, the muscle aches were like the return of an old friend. She remembered a time when the aches had been evidence of a hard afternoon's practice in Madame's class—proof that she was stretching herself beyond her previous limits and accomplishing things she'd never dreamed of before.

I've missed it, she thought with sudden astonishment as she performed a series of graceful ballet turns across the room. Oh, she didn't miss the ballet lessons with the infamous Madame. She didn't miss Madame's temperamental yelling. But she did miss the dancing. It felt good to be back in her tights and leotard, and it felt wonderful to be dancing again. She twirled around the living room, her body recalling the steps with ease. *Why do I feel so good about ballet now, and I felt so bad about it when I quit,* she asked herself as she moved. But deep down in her heart, she already knew the answer. *No more pressure,* she thought gleefully. *I don't have to dance to please Madame or Mom, or anyone. Just me!* she thought, leaping clear across the living room floor.

Later that afternoon, Chrissy and Caroline decided to treat themselves to a late lunch at the deli. They had just gotten their orders and sat down when Caroline groaned beneath her breath. "Uh oh, here comes trouble."

Chrissy looked up to see Madeleine Walsh making her way toward their table. "I thought she was your friend," Chrissy said curiously.

"She is, Chrissy, but I know she's going to ask me all kinds of details about my date last night with Bart. What am I going to do?" Caroline looked at Chrissy worriedly.

Chrissy gave her cousin a smile of utter confidence. "Just leave it all to me."

"Cara, I'm so glad I ran into you. I was going to call you later today." Madeleine grinned, gracefully seating herself at the girls' table. "I've been dying to know all day how things went with you and Bart last night."

"Uh . . . they went just fine . . ." Caroline said faintly.

"Did you like him? Are you going out again?"

"Uh . . . we're going out again tonight," Caroline said hesitantly.

"Oh, I knew it, I just knew it," Madeleine exclaimed in delight. "I just knew you and Bart would be perfect for each other, and I'm never wrong about these things!" She leaned toward Caroline eagerly. "So tell me all! I want to hear every little detail about your date last night!"

Caroline looked at Chrissy, a gleam of panic in her eyes.

"Oh, you won't be able to get any details out of Cara about last night," Chrissy said. "I've been trying to get her to tell me about her date all morning, but she keeps telling me it's just too special to talk about right now."

Madeleine looked at Caroline with total understanding. "I know just how you feel, Cara. I felt the same way when I first started dating James. I thought he was so wonderful and special, and I felt like if I talked about him to anyone, I'd somehow jinx it all." She smiled and gave Caroline an impulsive hug. "This just proves to me how positively right I was about you and Bart being so perfect for each other. Well, I've got to be on my way." She stood up and smiled at Chrissy and Caroline. "Oh, I feel just like Cupid," she exclaimed. Then waggling her fingers in good-bye, she left the deli.

"Phew," Caroline expelled a relieved sigh, then grinned at Chrissy. "We're terrible."

"I know, isn't it fun?" Chrissy asked mischievously. "Do you think she'll be upset when she finds out her Cupid's arrows hit the wrong girl?"

Caroline grinned at her cousin. "I think we'd better hope that you can keep on acting like me, because if Bart and Madeleine ever find out what's going on, we're two dead ducks!"

"Quack, quack," Chrissy breathed softly, causing both girls to dissolve into a fit of giggles.

Chapter 9

With Caroline's help, Chrissy dressed for her second date with Bart Reed. When she was finished, she looked at her reflection in the dresser mirror. She was wearing one of Caroline's Laura Ashley dresses with a muted, floral print, a belt at the middle, and a full, flowing skirt. Caroline had helped her twist her blond hair on top of her head, leaving loose tendrils to frame her face.

"Cara, are you sure I'm not too dressed up for an evening in the park?" Chrissy asked her cousin worriedly.

"Not at all," Caroline reassured her. "You look feminine and pretty. It's exactly what I would have chosen to wear if I were going." She gave Chrissy an encouraging smile.

Chrissy pointed down to her shoes. "What

about these old flats? Do they look okay?"

Caroline followed Chrissy's gaze. "Well, they are a bit worn, but they look nice with that dress. And with your hair up like that, you look like you stepped right out of one of Shakespeare's plays. I'm sure Bart will think you look charming." Caroline smiled again as the doorbell rang.

Chrissy smoothed down her skirt, gave her cousin a nervous grin, then went to open the door for Bart. Bart's approval of her outfit was evident in his sparkling eyes the minute Chrissy opened the door. Chrissy was impressed by the way he looked, too. Bart wore a pair of the latest style acid-washed jeans and a deep golden sweater that seemed to bring out the golden lights in his brown eyes. *How is it possible for me to feel so weak-kneed and breathless just by looking at him?* she wondered.

"Hi Cara," he said.

Chrissy just stared at him as if in a trance. "Oh, um, hi Bart," she stammered at last.

"Do you mind if I come in?" Bart asked. Chrissy stepped aside to let him into the Kirby apartment. "I'd really like to meet your parents," he went on.

"Uh ... my parents aren't here. Nobody's home. Why?" she asked hesitantly, praying that Caroline wouldn't slam a door or drop something in the bedroom.

"I was really hoping to be able to meet your father," Bart said with disappointment. "I'd like to talk to him about his work," he explained, as Chrissy quickly led him out of the apartment.

"Uh . . . Dad stays pretty busy most of the time. Maybe we can plan some other night for you to meet him," she said vaguely as they walked down the steps toward his car. *Mama mia*, she thought, *this keeps getting more and more complicated. Now he wants to meet my father!*

"When?" Bart asked the minute they'd settled into the plush seats of his sports car.

"When what?" Chrissy looked at him blankly.

"When could we set up a night for me to come over and meet your parents?" He smiled at her, the warm, beautiful smile that made Chrissy's heart flip-flop in her chest. "I don't want you to think I'm pushy or anything," he apologized.

"Oh, I don't," Chrissy murmured breathlessly, wondering how something as simple as his smile could make her feel like a bowl of quivering, jittery Jell-O.

"How about one night next week, like Wednesday night?" He smiled at her again.

"Sure, Wednesday night would be fine," she agreed without thinking, still mesmerized by his attractive smile.

"Great!" He reached over and gave her hand a warm, gentle squeeze. "I'm really looking forward to meeting them."

Chrissy smiled at him weakly, feeling almost sick to her stomach. *Oh, Cara*, she thought to herself, *you helped me get into this mess, I just hope you'll help me get out of it!*

As Bart removed his hand from hers and started the car, Chrissy looked out the window toward the Kirby apartment. *I wonder how Uncle Richard and Aunt Edith will feel about being my parents for a night,* she asked herself. She only hoped her aunt and uncle had as good a sense of humor as she and Caroline did!

"I saw your mother's picture in the newspaper this morning," Chrissy commented as Bart smoothly maneuvered his car through the heavy traffic.

Bart nodded. "The cultural center committee. It's Mother's pet project. She is very excited about it."

"It sounds like a pretty big responsibility," Chrissy said.

"It is, in fact it is one of the biggest projects Mother has ever worked on. The center will be enormous—large enough to house an auditorium, an art gallery, and a musical hall of fame. The overall cost for the project is two and a half million dollars." He laughed. "Mother definitely has her work cut out for her as chairperson of the fund-raising committee."

"Gosh." Chrissy breathed. It seemed strange to her that people would spend so much money to put up a big cultural center when they already had theaters and auditoriums and museums to do the same job. Why didn't Bart's mother work on a committee to raise funds for all the homeless people in the city? Chrissy wondered. She knew she couldn't ask Bart that question, though. *Certainly Caroline would never ask him a question like that,* she thought as she settled back in her seat.

The park where the Shakespeare reading was to take place was small, but to Chrissy it was beautiful. Here was the fresh, clean, smell she had missed, the smell of lush green grass and green-leaved tress. *How I would love to kick off my shoes and run barefoot through the grass,* she mused, remembering the feel of the thick Iowa grass beneath her toes. *But that is a very un-Caroline thing to do,* she reminded herself, *and I must remember that I am Caroline Kirby from San Francisco and not Chrissy Madden from Danbury, Iowa.* She consciously took small, lady-like steps as she and Bart walked across the park. In the center of the park a wooden platform had been constructed and a small crowd of people were already seated in the grass in front of it.

"Is this all right?" Bart asked as they stopped behind a couple sitting on a picnic blanket.

"Fine," Chrissy answered.

Bart frowned. "I didn't even think to bring a blanket with me." He looked worriedly at Chrissy's clothes.

"Don't worry. I really don't mind sitting on the grass," she said as she sat down and smiled up at him brightly.

He grinned and sat down next to her. "You're a good sport, Cara Kirby." He reached over and took her hand in his.

For a little while they simply sat quietly, watching as more people arrived and settled themselves on the grass in front of the platform. Before long the park buzzed with the sound of people laughing and talking as they waited for the reading to begin.

"It's nice out here, isn't it," Bart said softly.

"Yes," Chrissy agreed. "Although it's sort of noisy," she commented as the couple behind them laughed loudly and a group of people called to their friends who sat several feet away.

"Yeah, but it's a nice kind of noise," Bart said thoughtfully, causing Chrissy to look at him curiously. "My house is always so quiet. My parents are gone so much of the time and that just leaves me, the housekeeper, and the gardener." He grinned at her. "And sometimes I think they wear silencers on their shoes."

Chrissy smiled. "I guess it must be lonely being an only child."

Bart looked at her in surprise. "But you should know about being an only child," he said.

Chrissy flushed inwardly, cursing her own stupidity. "Oh, I do," she said hurriedly. "It's just that since my cousin, Chrissy, came to live with me, it's not so lonely anymore."

"There are lots of times when I've wished my parents would've had more kids." Bart confessed. "You know, to take some of the responsibility off me."

"What do you mean?" Chrissy asked curiously.

"Well, sometimes it seems like all my parents' hopes and dreams are all tied up in me, and it puts a lot of pressure on me to always do the things that I think will make them happy." He smiled at her. "But I guess you know all about that, too."

Chrissy nodded thoughtfully. No, she didn't really understand the sort of pressure that was placed on an only child. With three brothers, she didn't have to worry. *I can't very well tell that to Bart,* she thought. *But now I understand better why Caroline took dancing lessons for such a long time to make Aunt Edith happy.* She thought of her cousin with new respect, and smiled at Bart. There was more to Bart than just his good looks, and she wanted to learn more about him.

"Are you chilly?" Bart asked. Chrissy was about to say no, but was grateful she didn't when Bart put his arm around her and drew her closer to him. It felt good to have his arm snugly around her shoulders, and it seemed completely natural for her to rest her head against his firm shoulder. His sweater was soft against her cheek and smelled of his pleasant, tangy cologne.

"A good crowd has turned out for the reading," Bart said.

Chrissy stretched her neck to look around without leaving the warmth of Bart's shoulder. Sure enough, at least a hundred people were seated around the platform.

"Yes, there are a lot of people here," Chrissy said, surprised to see how many people had shown up to hear the Shakespearean reading. *I always thought that Shakespeare was really boring*, she thought, *but he must be pretty popular.*

As the readings got under way, Chrissy realized she had been right all along. Shakespeare was boring, boring, boring! She tried to concentrate, but all the words seemed jumbled together in one long monotone. The cool night air caressed her face, smelling of spring and salt from the bay, and Bart's arm was warm and cozy around her. *I sure am glad Caroline is content with her letters from Luke,* she thought. *Otherwise, I wouldn't be here now with a living, breathing, wonderful boy sitting right next to me!*

Chrissy snuggled closer to Bart. *I really feel like taking my shoes off,* she thought again. *Then I would be completely one hundred percent comfortable.* She wiggled her feet inside her shoes. *No, I'd better not—not if I'm supposed to be Caroline.*

But who would ever know if you took them off? a small voice said deep inside her. It was dark where she and Bart were seated, and nobody would ever know if her shoes were on her feet or off. What difference would it make? She could slip them back on when it was time to go and nobody would even know they had been off. Almost without moving a muscle, she managed to kick off both shoes, immediately enjoying the feel of the cool, damp grass beneath her bare feet.

As she sat there, enjoying the feel of the grass

beneath her feet, and comfortably resting her head on Bart's firm, strong shoulder, she found her thoughts drifting far away from the speakers on the platform.

She had really enjoyed her ballet lesson with Caroline that morning. She hadn't realized before that ballet dancing could be so much fun. Even though she had been terribly sore immediately following the lesson, soaking in the hot tub had taken away most of the aches and pains. Now she was really looking forward to her next lesson. *Wouldn't it be something if I really got to be good at ballet,* she mused, not even hearing the droning voice of the speaker up on the stage as her thoughts continued. *Wouldn't it be great if I practiced and practiced and got to be as good a ballet dancer as Caroline. Wouldn't Caroline be proud of me? Wouldn't Bart be proud of me?*

She closed her eyes, imagining herself floating gracefully across a polished stage. She was wearing a beautiful, white filmy costume that flowed around her as she performed sharp, crisp ballet turns and high, breathtaking leaps in the air. As she danced across the stage, she could see Bart watching her from the wings, his brown eyes glowing with pride and in his arms a dozen long-stemmed red roses. Caroline was sitting out in the audience, shouting "bravo" and clapping enthusiastically. Chrissy's dance came to an end, she bowed regally, hearing the thunderous applause of the audience.

"Caroline . . . Caroline!"

Chrissy jerked upright at the sound of Bart's voice. How could she have dozed off like that? She could see several people around them looking at her, hiding small smiles. "What's the matter?" she asked Bart, hoping she didn't sound as sleepy as she felt.

Bart's eyes glinted in the dark and he grinned at her in amusement. "You were snoring."

"I wasn't!" Chrissy's eyes widened in horror.

"Then it was the best imitation of a snore I've ever heard," Bart's shoulders shook with laughter.

Chrissy could feel the heat rise in her cheeks. *How embarrassing!* she thought. *That is about the most un-Cara-like thing I could have done.*

As usual, though, Chrissy couldn't help but see the funny side. She elbowed Bart lightly in his stomach. "Stop laughing," she whispered with a barely stifled giggle.

"I can't help it," Bart gasped, his shoulders shaking once again.

For the rest of the reading, Bart and Chrissy couldn't look at each other without gulping back bursts of uncontrollable giggles.

When the readings finally came to an end, Bart turned to her, his eyes sparkling merrily. "I never knew Shakespeare could be so funny," he chuckled, rising to his feet and holding out his hand to help her up. "Ready to go?"

Chrissy nodded and started to get up, then stopped. She didn't have her shoes on. She felt around in the grass with her feet and found one shoe, which she quickly slipped on. But where was her other shoe?

"What's the matter?" Bart asked, still leaning over and waiting for her to stand up.

"I . . . uh . . . I can't find one of my shoes," she confessed with a giggle.

"You can't find your shoe?" Bart's deep voice was full of puzzlement. "Isn't it on your foot?"

His logical question made Chrissy giggle once again. "I kicked them off during the reading, and it's so dark out here I can't find one of them." She got down on her hands and knees and began sweeping her arm out before her.

"I can't believe we're doing this," Bart's laughter rumbled pleasantly as he crouched down next to her to help search through the grass.

It was so dark in the park she could barely see her hand in front of her face, when Chrissy suddenly realized that everyone else had gone home. They were totally alone in the park. "Bart . . . ?" She turned her head to look at him at the same time he turned to look at her. They both yelped as their heads collided in the darkness.

It was Chrissy who began to giggle first. Here she was, pretending to be a proper, well-bred young lady attending a Shakespearean reading. First she had fallen asleep and snored, now she was crawling around on her hands and knees with a proper, great-looking guy, looking for one of her shoes!

In seconds Bart had caught Chrissy's giggles,

and before long they were both laying flat on their backs in the cool, damp grass laughing hysterically.

"Okay, now Cara," Bart finally said, sitting up and getting control of himself. "Now where could your shoe be? It didn't just get up and walk away!"

Bart's joke made Chrissy burst into another fit of uncontrollable giggling. "You sound just like my mother," she said, gasping for breath. "Who knows what happened to my shoe, maybe somebody accidentally folded it up with their blanket." She stood up, standing crookedly with one shoe on and one shoe off. "They are an old pair, anyway. Let's just forget about it."

"Are you sure?" Bart asked, also rising to his feet.

"I'm positive." Chrissy took off the one shoe she was wearing.

"Well, I can't let you walk barefoot all the way to the car," Bart said thoughtfully, moving closer to her.

"There really isn't much in the way of alternatives, unless you want to give me your shoes to wear and you walk barefoot to the car."

"I can think of one alternative." Without warning, he scooped her up in his arms. "This way I don't have to worry about your stepping on a piece of glass or something," he said softly as he carried her toward the parking lot.

Now Chrissy's face really burned with embarrassment. She had so wanted to be exactly like

Caroline tonight, level headed and ladylike, and instead she was being carried like a baby across the park because once again she had managed to do something impulsive and stupid!

Although, she had to admit, it was very nice to be carried in Bart's arms. She wrapped her arms lightly around his neck, enjoying the way his dark hair curled slightly at the nape. *At least there were some advantages in doing something very Chrissy-like,* she thought with a small smile. *Still, I've got to be more careful,* she warned herself, *too many of these mess-ups and Bart won't like me. Or worse, he will guess that I'm not the real Caroline Kirby.*

"Here we go, fair maiden, delivered safe and sound," Bart said as they reached his car. Gently he set her down on the pavement of the parking area.

"Thank you, kind prince," Chrissy replied with a grin, but then she sobered. "Bart, I'm really sorry," she began hesitantly. "It was really stupid of me to kick off my shoes in the first place. I can't imagine what made me take them off." She looked down at the pavement with a blush of embarrassment.

"Hey, Cara." He touched her chin and tilted her head toward him. "Please don't be embarrassed. It isn't very often that I get to crawl around in the grass with a pretty girl. I have to admit, I had a lot of fun." He looked at her thoughtfully. "I knew from what Madeleine told me about you that we would have a lot of things in common, but you are somehow different than what I expected." He leaned down and his lips met hers in a sweet, tender kiss.

Chrissy was thrilled by his kiss, but his words caused a cold clutch of panic to grab her heart. She wanted to be exactly what he had expected her to be! She wanted to be Caroline Kirby!

Chapter 10

For the hundredth time Wednesday evening, Chrissy slowly walked around the Kirby living room, making certain there were absolutely no clues that might reveal her true identity. The two portraits of Caroline that were usually on display in the room were now resting comfortably in a drawer, carefully hidden and out of sight. Everything was ready, and at any moment Bart would be arriving to meet her "parents."

Chrissy sat down on the sofa, carefully straightening out her new gray skirt so that it wouldn't wrinkle. She leaned forward and used the bottom of the peach-colored sweater she wore to wipe a speck of dust off the coffee table, then settled back and looked around her with a sense of satisfaction.

It had taken Chrissy and Caroline two whole days of pleading to convince Richard and Edith Kirby to play the role of Chrissy's parents.

"Absolutely not!" Uncle Richard had said when Caroline and Chrissy had first brought up the idea. "Don't get me involved in your feminine schemes!"

"Oh please, Uncle Richard, just for this one night," Chrissy begged.

"Come on, Dad, the only reason Bart wants to meet you is because he admires your work so much," Caroline added.

Uncle Richard shook his finger at his daughter. "Don't think flattery will get you anywhere!" He grinned.

"Girls, we really shouldn't get involved in all this," Aunt Edith had said, although her eyes had twinkled with amusement.

And on it had gone, with the girls begging and pleading. Finally, their pleas and her aunt and uncle's good humor had won out—on the condition that it would only be this once.

Uncle Richard and Aunt Edith were now in the kitchen, arranging a platter of bakery goodies they'd bought to serve when Bart arrived. Caroline was in the girls' bedroom studying. The cousins had agreed that Caroline would only make an appearance if it couldn't be avoided. And if that happened, she'd have to make her acting debut as Chrissy Madden from Danbury, Iowa.

Once again Chrissy stood up and walked

around the living room restlessly, wishing Bart would hurry up and get here so she could get this visit over. She wanted everything to go perfectly, and more than anything, she wanted Bart to keep on liking her.

After the Shakespearean reading Saturday night, she and Bart had gone to a hamburger drive-in, the only place they could think of to go since Chrissy was barefooted. In the privacy of Bart's car, over hamburgers and soft drinks, they had talked. Actually, Chrissy had done more listening than talking, afraid that if she spoke too much she would somehow manage to say the wrong things and Bart wouldn't like her anymore.

She hated to keep deceiving Bart, but she didn't see any other solution if she wanted to keep seeing him. *Maybe if I go out with him a few more times, he will like me so much it won't matter that I'm not Caroline,* she thought, jumping nervously as her Aunt Edith entered the living room.

"Well, we have three different kinds of cookies and some *petits fours* to serve to your young man this evening," she smiled brightly at Chrissy. "And Uncle Richard is in the bedroom now putting on a tie. I told him he should look more professional."

"Thanks, Aunt Edith," Chrissy said, then caught herself. "I mean, thanks Mom." She grinned at her aunt, then froze as the doorbell rang. "That must be him," she said anxiously, looking at her aunt with widened blue eyes.

"Relax honey." Her aunt gave her a quick, warm hug. "Your Uncle Richard and I won't do anything to give your game away." She straightened up and smiled at Chrissy. "Now Caroline, don't you think you should go open the door for Bart?"

Chrissy gave her aunt a grateful smile, then taking a big, deep breath, she went to open the door for Bart. As usual, Bart looked absolutely wonderful. He was dressed in dark brown cords and a rust-colored polo shirt that emphasized his broad shoulders, and in his hands he held two large bouquets of freshly cut flowers.

"Hi." She smiled up at him, wondering if she would ever get used to his good looks. Would her heart always pound so frantically whenever she looked at him? Would she always feel like she was melting away whenever he smiled at her and made the lines at the corner of his brown eyes crinkle so attractively?

"Hi. These are for you," he said, smiling and handing her a bouquet of flowers.

"Thank you, they're beautiful," she murmured, taking the bouquet and burying her nose in the flowers to breathe in their sweet fragrance.

Bart smiled at her in amusement. "Are you going to invite me in or are we going to stand here in the doorway and visit all evening?"

Chrissy blushed. "Please, come in," she said hurriedly, ushering him inside and closing the door behind him. "Bart, this is my mother, Edith

Kirby," Chrissy introduced her aunt as she and Bart entered the living room.

"Hello Bart, it's nice meeting you." Aunt Edith gave him a friendly smile.

"It's nice to meet you, Mrs. Kirby. Oh, these are for you." He held out the other bouquet of flowers.

"How very nice." Edith Kirby took the flowers and handed them to Chrissy. "Caroline, why don't you take these into the kitchen and put them in a vase of water while I get your unc . . . father and introduce him to Bart."

Chrissy nodded and took the flowers into the kitchen. *It was really nice of Bart to bring flowers,* she thought, opening up the cabinets in search of a vase. *And not only for me, but for Aunt, I mean Mom, as well.*

At last Chrissy found a pretty crystal vase in the very last cabinet. As she filled the vase with water, she thought of her own mother, and wondered what Ingrid Madden would think of a boy like Bart. Chrissy knew her mother wouldn't be overly impressed by Bart's good looks, nor would she be impressed by his family's wealth. She was much too down-to-earth for that. Aunt Edith seemed to like Bart, and Chrissy knew that her mother respected her sister's judgment. But Bart's main asset was the fact that he seemed to know exactly where he was going with his life—he had definite goals and dreams for his future. *And he's so nice,* Chrissy thought with a dreamy sigh.

"Oh rats!" She stifled a squeal as the water reached the top of the vase and began to splatter in all directions. Quickly she reached out and shut off the faucet. She grabbed a dish towel from next to the sink and patted the wet splotches on the front of her sweater, until it was reasonably dry, then ran the towel across the countertop.

I've been in here for ages, Chrissy thought, feeling nervous. *I hope Aunt Edith and Uncle Richard haven't slipped up.*

Swiftly Chrissy stuck the flowers in the vase and carefully carried it back into the living room, where she found her aunt and uncle sitting in their large armchairs and Bart sitting on the sofa, looking comfortable and relaxed. Chrissy set the vase of flowers on the coffee table, then perched herself on the edge of the sofa, nervously looking at the other three in the room.

"I was just telling your parents how much we enjoyed the ballet last Friday night," Bart explained. "*Coppelia* has always been one of my favorites."

"Oh yes, it was wonderful." Chrissy nodded and let out a small sigh of relief. So far the plan was working!

"I keep trying to convince Caroline to dance for me," Bart said to Aunt Edith and Uncle Richard with a smile. "After all the years of training she's had, I'm sure she's very good. I really would love to see her dance."

"Oh, I doubt very much that you'll ever talk Caroline into dancing for you." Mrs. Kirby's eyes twinkled merrily. "Caroline is very shy about dancing in front of other people."

"Very shy . . ." Uncle Richard echoed, glancing at Chrissy as if he were trying not to laugh.

Bart looked over at Chrissy with a warm smile. "I know Caroline is modest, but I've also heard that she's very talented. Some day I'll be lucky enough to see her dance."

Chrissy saw her Uncle Richard hide a smile with the back of his hand, and her Aunt Edith looked like she was going to burst into laughter.

"Who knows, Bart, maybe you will manage to talk me into dancing for you some time," Chrissy said. Now it was her turn to hold in her laughter at the astonished expressions of her aunt and uncle. *After all,* she thought, *Caroline has given me three ballet lessons already, and I'll just keep on practicing until I'm good enough to dance for Bart!*

"Bart, I read in the newspaper that your mother has been elected chairperson of the fund-raising committee for the new cultural center. I imagine that will keep her quite busy." Chrissy's aunt quickly changed the subject.

"Yes, it's going to be called the Metropolitan Cultural Center, and Mother is very excited about it. When I left to come over here this evening, she was already in the middle of planning an auction." Bart smiled at Mrs. Kirby. "I imagine she'll be contacting your gallery soon to see if you'll donate some artwork."

"Well, you can tell her that we'll be happy to help," Mrs. Kirby replied.

"An auction, what fun!" Chrissy exclaimed brightly, recalling all the auctions she had been to back home in Danbury. Everyone in the town would turn out for an auction, and there was nothing more fun that sitting in the shade of a tree, sipping a soft drink, and listening to the chatter of a good, professional auctioneer. "I always wonder how the auctioneer can talk so fast."

"I think mother is planning on a silent auction," Bart explained.

"Oh, I see," Chrissy said, but she really didn't. What in the heck was a silent auction, she wondered. An auction wasn't an auction without a loud-talking, tongue-twisting auctioneer. At a silent auction did the auctioneer just keep silent and point to different items? *They sure do things differently in San Francisco*, she thought in amazement.

"Mr. Kirby, I've been wanting to talk to you about your work. I'm interested in doing the same kind of work someday," Bart turned to Chrissy's uncle with interest.

Chrissy found herself beginning to relax as her Uncle Richard and Bart began to discuss journalism. *Things are going really well,* she thought happily as she listened to Bart and her Uncle Richard talk animatedly on a subject they both enjoyed. She smiled as her Aunt Edith caught her eye and winked. *I am so lucky to have such a wonderful aunt and uncle,* she thought. *They are really doing me a big favor by going along with my Caroline act.* Thinking about Caroline, she hoped her cousin wouldn't have to make an appearance. *Caroline would never be able to act like me, and if he sees us both together, Bart might realize that I'm not the real Caroline Kirby.*

It seemed as if Bart had been able to read her mind, because he suddenly turned to her, a curious expression on his face. "I thought you told me that your cousin lived with you. You know, the cousin from Iowa that you told me about."

"She does," Chrissy said.

"Is she home? I would really like to meet her," Bart said, smiling at Chrissy. "You told me how close you two are."

"Chrissy's not here. She's um . . ." But before Chrissy could think of an excuse, Caroline entered the living room grinning widely.

"Holy Mazoly, so this is Bart!" She stomped over and grabbed Bart's hand, pumping it up and down enthusiastically. "It's good to finally meet you, Bart."

Chrissy's mouth dropped open and her blue eyes opened wide as she stared at her cousin in horror!

Chapter 11

Caroline was dressed in a pair of Chrissy's faded blue overalls, with one of Chrissy's tattered, paint-speckled sweat-shirts beneath. Her blond hair was pulled up into two pigtails, one slightly higher than the other, and tiny freckles had been painted across the bridge of her nose. Her entire face was engulfed by a wide, open grin.

All she needs is a missing front tooth and a pitchfork and she'll look like a real hillbilly, Chrissy thought. She blinked slowly in the hope that when she opened her eyes she would find that the girl in front of her was just a hallucination. *No, she's definitely real. If that's Cara's best imitation of me, she's way off the mark. I don't look like that!*

She turned to her Uncle Richard and Aunt

Edith, outraged that they hadn't let her in on the joke, but one look at their faces and Chrissy realized that her aunt and uncle had no part in planning Caroline's ridiculous disguise. Uncle Richard's face was a brilliant red and his shoulders were shaking with silent laughter. And Aunt Edith was sucking in her cheeks so hard to keep from laughing that she looked like a fish out of water.

"Caroline has been telling me all about you," Caroline said brightly, finally releasing Bart's hand and plopping down on the sofa between him and Chrissy. "Caroline told me all about the ballet you took her to. She sure does like all that ballerina junk. She also told me all about that Shakespeare thing you guys went to. Cara likes all that kind of stuff, but I think that Shakespeare guy is really hard to understand, don't you?" Caroline paused a moment and looked around the room at everyone. "Oops," she clapped her hand over her mouth and smiled sheepishly. "I guess I'm running at the mouth again. I always talk too much when I meet somebody new."

"How do you like living here in San Francisco?" Bart asked, looking at Caroline with a sort of dazed expression as if he couldn't quite grasp what he was seeing. "San Francisco must be quite different from your hometown in Iowa."

"Different!" Caroline squealed with delight.

Bart jumped in surprise, while Chrissy clenched her teeth in anger. "That's not really what I'm like," she wanted to shout, but she didn't dare.

"Holy cow!" Caroline continued loudly. "There is no way to compare Danbury to San Francisco." She leaned forward with an eager look on her face. "Here in San Francisco, you have the Golden Gate Bridge, and Chinatown, and the beach, and so many different movie theaters. Why, here a person could go to a different movie theater every week and not see the same movie for a whole year!"

"I never thought about it before, but I guess you're right." Bart smiled at Caroline.

"Back in Danbury, all there is to do is sit around and watch the grass grow," Caroline continued.

"That's not true," Chrissy protested hotly, then blushed as Bart turned and looked at her in surprise. "I visited Danbury last spring with Chrissy. It's a wonderful little town with lots of things to do," Chrissy blushed again, knowing it sounded rather suspicious for her to be defending Danbury, but she couldn't just sit quietly by and let Caroline make fun of her.

"I can't imagine you being on a farm." Bart smiled warmly at Chrissy.

"Oh, Cara fit right in at the farm," Caroline giggled. "It was almost as if she'd been born there!"

"Caroline is very adaptable," Uncle Richard said, trying to keep a straight face. Chrissy looked at her Uncle Richard gratefully, then glared at her cousin.

"So Bart, when is your mother planning to hold this big auction?" Once again Aunt Edith quickly changed the subject.

"I think she is going to try to plan it for some-time around Easter," Bart told Mrs. Kirby.

"Oh, I love Easter," Caroline exploded enthusi-astically. "Back home we always have a great big Easter-egg hunt. My mom and dad always hide hundreds of colored eggs all over the farm." She giggled, ignoring the daggers that were shooting out of Chrissy's eyes at her. "My folks always make sure they hide plenty of the colored eggs in the hen house, so Easter is the one day the chicken eggs get gathered without any com-plaints!"

"Do you have other animals on your farm besides chickens?" Bart asked politely.

"Holy Mazoly, do we have animals! It's like a regular zoo on our farm!" Caroline grinned at Bart, a huge grin that made her look exactly like a real country bumpkin. "We've got dogs and cats, and cows and pigs. Why, I've got the cutest little pet piglet, he sleeps with me every single night!" She grinned again, making the painted-on freckles on her nose dance up and down.

"Chrissy, would you like to help me bring in the cookies and tea from the kitchen?" Chrissy slid off the sofa and glared pointedly at her cousin.

"Sure, Cara." Caroline jumped up and patted Bart on his knee. "We'll be back in a jiffy," she said, then followed Chrissy into the kitchen.

"Caroline Kirby, what on earth do you think

you are doing?" Chrissy hissed the moment the two girls were alone in the kitchen.

"What do you mean?" Caroline gave her cousin an innocent smile.

"Don't play dumb with me! You know exactly what I mean," Chrissy snapped. "What is the deal with this ridiculous getup?" She tweaked one of Caroline's pigtails.

"I'm doing exactly what you wanted me to do," Caroline replied with a mischievous grin. "I'm being you!"

"No, you're not!" Chrissy protested heatedly, placing the earthenware pitcher containing the spiced tea in the microwave.

"Yes, I am." Caroline returned lightly. She reached over and punched the proper buttons on the microwave, making it hum into action.

"That is not the way I am," Chrissy protested. "You make me seem like a total hick!"

Caroline placed five cups and saucers onto a serving tray. "Chrissy, when you first came here, you were a total hick!"

"But, I was never as bad as that." Chrissy looked at her cousin hesitantly. "Was I?"

"Well, I may be exaggerating a bit," Caroline confessed with a small laugh, then added teasingly, "but just a little bit!"

"A little bit ... 'I've got the cutest little pet piglet and I sleep with it every night.'" Chrissy couldn't help laughing, as she mimicked Caroline.

"You call that a little bit?" She shook her head

in frustration, but she was no longer angry. "I'm just surprised you weren't struck by a bolt of lightning for telling such tall tales!"

"That part about the pet pig was pretty good, wasn't it?" Caroline said.

Chrissy simply shook her head again, and took the pitcher of hot tea from the microwave with an oven mitt. Carefully she placed the pitcher on the tray.

"You have to admit one thing," Caroline grinned at her cousin. "I should receive an Academy Award for my expert performance."

"Here, I'll give you the official Chrissy Madden award for your expert performance." Chrissy stuck out her tongue and blew her cousin a loud raspberry.

"Come on." Caroline giggled. "Let's see if I can keep up this act for the second half of the show." She picked up the serving tray and left the kitchen. "Holy Mazoly, this tea is hot!" Chrissy heard her cousin exclaim. Stifling a giggle, Chrissy grabbed the platter of baked goodies and went out to face her cousin's encore performance.

"That smells delicious," Bart commented as Chrissy carefully poured him a cup of the spiced tea.

"It's a secret family recipe," Mrs. Kirby said.

"Guaranteed to curl your toes and grow hair on your chest!" Caroline exclaimed with a bright smile.

At that, Uncle Richard was instantly gripped by

a coughing spasm. Finally he cleared his throat and stood up, refusing to look at either Chrissy or Caroline. "If you kids will excuse me, I have some work to finish." He smiled at Bart. "Bart, it was a pleasure to meet you."

"Thank you, sir, and I appreciate your advice," Bart said, shaking Uncle Richard's hand. Then Uncle Richard disappeared down the hall.

"And I have some things to attend to also." Aunt Edith stood up and smiled. "Bart, I enjoyed meeting you. Please tell your mother that the gallery would be happy to donate something for the auction. Good night, kids."

"Good night," the three echoed as Aunt Edith left the room.

"Your parents are really nice people," Bart said, sitting back down on the sofa.

"Oh, Aunt Edith and Uncle Richard are wonderful people," Caroline beamed. "They treat me just as if I was their very own daughter!"

"Chrissy, wouldn't you like a cookie?" Chrissy asked Caroline, hoping that if her cousin's mouth was full, she wouldn't be able to say anything.

"You know me, Cara, I never pass up an opportunity to eat!" Caroline grabbed a handful of cookies and popped one in her mouth, then looked at Bart and Chrissy expectantly. "Oh, I guess maybe you two would like some time alone," she said. "I'll just get back to my studying. Goodness knows I need all the study time I can get." She stood up and grabbed a couple of *petits fours*. "I just love these little cakes—we didn't have anything like this in Danbury!" she explained. "See you guys later." She grinned broadly, then disappeared down the hallway toward the bedroom.

Chrissy turned to Bart and smiled in relief. They had done it! They had actually managed to carry off the switch of identities for the entire evening! Now she could relax and enjoy spending the rest of the time alone with Bart.

"Your cousin is ... uh ... very interesting," Bart said, taking a cookie from the platter.

Chrissy laughed. "That's an understatement!" She shook her head in wonder. If she hadn't seen Caroline's country bumpkin act with her own eyes, she would have never believed it! Shy, reserved Caroline Kirby, holy mazolying and clomping around in tacky overalls in front of a virtual stranger? Even after seeing it, Chrissy still found it hard to believe!

"I'll bet she's a lot of fun to live with," Bart said, biting into his cookie. "Is she always so ... bubbly?"

Chrissy hesitated for a moment before answering. *It's strange to sit back and watch somebody else act like you, then see if you think you really are the way they made you appear,* she thought. Caroline had exaggerated a lot of Chrissy's personality traits, but Chrissy knew that all the things Caroline had said and done had been based on the truth.

"Yes," she finally answered with a small smile. "Most of the time I guess you could say that

Chrissy is pretty bubbly. But that's not a bad thing to be, is it?" She looked at Bart worriedly, not giving him a chance to respond. "She just gets excited about so many things. Everything is so new and exciting for her here in San Francisco, and she just isn't very good about hiding her feelings."

"Hey, Cara, you don't have to defend your cousin to me. I liked her!" Bart said, placing an arm around Chrissy's shoulders. "But, most of all, I like you."

Chrissy's heart fluttered in her chest. "I like you, too," she said softly.

"Good," he replied with a smile. "It's so much nicer when the girl you like, likes you back."

"I can't imagine you liking some girl and her not liking you back," Chrissy teased. "You don't look like a guy who has suffered too many major heartbreaks."

"Not too many." He grinned, looking at her curiously. "What about you? Have you suffered many broken hearts?"

Again Chrissy hesitated before answering. "I don't think I've ever suffered from a real broken heart," she replied. "My heart has been kicked around and bruised a bit, but never broken." Though Bart was the kind of guy who could sympathize, she could never mention Ben, the boy she had left behind in Danbury—not in her new role as Caroline from San Francisco.

Bart nodded in understanding. "I really like your home," he said, looking around the living

room with interest. "It has a nice, warm feel to it."
He laughed self-consciously. "I guess that sounds
sort of stupid."

"No, it doesn't," Chrissy assured him. She
sensed a certain wistfulness in Bart. She had
sensed it in the park when he had talked about
the silence of his house, and she sensed it again
now. *He's lonely,* she suddenly thought in amazement, *this nice, handsome, wonderful guy is
lonely.*

"I'm glad our blind date worked out so well,"
Bart said softly, leaning forward to give her a
tender kiss.

When they parted, Chrissy's heart was still
beating rapidly. She had an overwhelming desire
to tell him the truth, the whole truth. She liked
him too much to continue deceiving him by pretending to be Cara Kirby. *I'll explain everything
to him and we'll both laugh about it, then he'll tell
me it doesn't matter and we will go on from there,*
she thought hopefully. "Bart," she began. "I'm
really . . ."

"Wonderful," Bart finished her sentence for
her, his lips lowering toward hers for another
kiss, this one taking Chrissy's breath away. "And
I'm sure you are getting tired, too," he said as he
broke the kiss and stood up. "It is getting late and
it's a school night, so I really should be getting
home." He pulled her to her feet. "Come on and
walk me to my car." He put his arm around her
shoulder and together they walked out of the
apartment and down the stairs toward his car.

Tell him, a small voice said deep inside her. *Tell him that you are not really Caroline Kirby.* But it was the same small voice that had told her nobody would ever know if she kicked off her shoes at the Shakespeare reading, and she certainly wasn't eager to trust that voice again so soon.

"You know," Bart began as they approached his car. "I've been driving all my friends at Forsythe crazy talking about the great girl I met on a blind date." He grinned at her. "They're all getting pretty sick of the name of Caroline Kirby!"

Chrissy smiled weakly, knowing now that she could never tell him who she really was. She would just have to continue masquerading as Caroline Kirby and hope that somehow, someday, this whole mess would sort itself out!

"Cara, are you asleep?" Chrissy whispered as she crept into the dark bedroom.

"No, not yet. I just shut off the light. You can turn it back on if you want." Caroline's bed squeaked as she turned over to face Chrissy in the dark. "Did Bart go home?"

"Yeah," Chrissy answered absently. She didn't bother with the light, but pulled off the peach-colored sweater and dropped it to the floor.

"Did you guys have a fight or something?" Caroline asked.

"No, why?"

"I don't know, you just sound sort of glum," Caroline answered.

Chrissy stepped out of her gray skirt, allowing it to fall on top of the pile of dirty clothes at the foot of her bed. "I'm not glum really, I'm just sort of confused." She paused long enough to feel around on her bed until her hand found the flannel fabric of her nightgown. She pulled the nightgown over her head, crawled beneath the bedsheets, then continued. "I guess I'm just feeling sort of guilty about pretending to be you. I don't want to risk telling Bart the truth. He might get really mad and never want to see me again."

"Chrissy, the way I see it, you really only have two choices," Caroline said thoughtfully. "A) you can tell him the truth. Either Madeleine and Bart will never speak to either one of us again, or Bart might be really understanding and say he doesn't care, he likes you anyway. Or B) you can just continue pretending to be me."

"How about C) none of the above," Chrissy joked, then turned serious once again. "It would have been so much easier if Bart had turned out to be a total nerd. Then one date would have been the end of it."

"Well, he definitely is not a nerd, that's for sure," Caroline replied lightly.

"Are you sorry you gave him to me?" Chrissy asked, holding her breath anxiously. What if after meeting Bart tonight, Caroline suddenly became interested in him? Bart liked Chrissy because she was pretending to be Caroline Kirby.

Didn't that mean he would like the real Cara Kirby even more?

"I'm not a bit sorry," Caroline replied firmly, and Chrissy sighed with relief. "I told you before, I'm perfectly happy with Luke. In fact, I got another letter from him today." Caroline's voice was light with happiness. "Luke has already applied to Colorado University as well as other schools in Colorado, so there's a good chance that we'll at least be in the same state."

"Don't remind me of college, then you really will make me glum," Chrissy said gloomily.

Caroline smiled sympathetically in the darkness. "So, was Bart impressed by your country cousin?" she asked in an attempt to lighten the conversation.

Chrissy giggled. "I'm not sure how impressed Bart was, but *I* was certainly impressed. Although I was pretty angry at first. Honestly, Cara, if I hadn't seen it with my own eyes, I wouldn't have believed it!"

It was Caroline's turn to giggle. "I have to admit, it was harder than I thought it would be," she confessed. "It took me a long time to get up enough nerve to leave the bedroom."

"This trading places business is a real challenge, don't you think?" Chrissy replied. "Every minute I spend with Bart I have to be on my guard, watch every word I say and every move I make."

Caroline laughed. "And while I was pretending to be you, I had to do the exact opposite." She yawned sleepily. "All I know is that I never realized before how much energy it takes to be you. All that holy mazolying and high spirits is completely exhausting. I don't know how you do it every day!"

"I guess we've both realized how hard it is to be each other," Chrissy said thoughtfully.

"That's for sure," Caroline agreed. "So, what are you going to do about Bart? Are you going to tell him the truth or keep on pretending to be Caroline Kirby?"

There was a long pause before Chrissy answered, and when she did her voice was low and thoughtful. "Well, I've always heard that a little bit of guilt is good for the soul. I guess my soul is going to be in great shape. I think I'll go on feeling guilty and keep on pretending to be you."

"Just make sure you tell him your real name in time for the wedding invitations to be printed properly." Caroline teased sleepily.

"Oh, don't worry about that," Chrissy assured her with a sleepy yawn of her own. "If it ever comes to a wedding, there is no way I would ever let Bart Reed say 'I do' to Caroline Kirby." Chrissy yawned again. "Good night Caroline."

"Good night Chrissy." Caroline turned over and pulled the sheet up snugly around her neck.

The room was silent for just a moment, then Caroline heard a strange sound coming from Chrissy's bed. It was a sort of snorting, grunting sound. But when Caroline closed her eyes, Chrissy was once again silent. A moment later

Chrissy made the same noise again. "Chrissy, what on earth are you doing?" Caroline finally demanded impatiently.

"I'm making pig noises," Chrissy replied matter-of-factly.

"Why are you making pig noises?" Caroline asked with ill-concealed aggravation.

"I just thought you might be missing that cute, little pet piglet you sleep with every night back home," Chrissy explained with a burst of giggles, alternating with pig snorts. She squealed as Caroline's pillow sailed across the room and hit her square on her head. "Hey, watch out, you'll hurt your pet piglet!"

"If that piglet doesn't quiet down and let me get some sleep, it will be a slab of bacon before morning!" Caroline's giggles mingled with Chrissy's to fill the darkness of the bedroom.

Chapter 12

"Cara, can I borrow your black jacket to wear tonight?"

Caroline looked up from the letter she was writing to Luke, fighting down a feeling of slight resentment at Chrissy's request. It seemed as if in the past few weeks, Chrissy had completely abandoned her own wardrobe in favor of Caroline's more sedate clothes. "I thought you bought a new outfit to wear to the symphony tonight."

"I did!" Chrissy said brightly, turning around slowly to show off the slender black skirt and ruffled white blouse. "Doesn't it look great? It's exactly like something you would have bought." She frowned slightly. "But it really needs your black jacket to complete the look."

"I guess you can wear it," Caroline said finally with a heavy sigh. "But be careful with it, I've only worn it twice."

"Thanks, Cara, you're the greatest!" Chrissy grinned, grabbing the black jacket from the closet. "Oh, that must be Bart," she exclaimed as the doorbell rang. Quickly she pulled on the black jacket. "See ya later," she called as she ran out of the bedroom.

Caroline rolled over on her stomach and stared at the letter she had just begun to write to Luke.

Dear Luke,

    Chrissy has slowly begun to take over my entire life, and it's really making me mad. It started out with her pretending to be me on a date. At first it was fun, but not anymore. She borrows my clothes and doesn't even take care of them. She can be such a slob!

    She's doing all the things that I like to do, like going to museums, and operas, and foreign-film festivals. She's really driving me crazy!

Caroline stared at the letter, then slowly crumpled it up into a tiny ball. There was no way she could send a letter like that to Luke.

You're just jealous, Caroline Kirby, a small voice chided from deep inside her. *You're jealous because Chrissy has found somebody she really likes and they are doing things together while you sit home and wait for letters from your long-distance boyfriend. You're jealous because it's Saturday night and you're sitting home all alone while Chrissy is going to the symphony with Bart!*

But, that's not true, Caroline protested silently, getting up off her bed and going over to the bedroom window. She pulled the curtain aside and stared out blankly. *The problem isn't that I'm jealous of Chrissy and Bart, the problem is Chrissy herself!*

Caroline sighed and turned away from the window, her stomach rumbling with hunger.

Her parents had gone out for supper, and with Chrissy also gone, Caroline was on her own for the evening meal. She wandered into the kitchen and looked in the refrigerator, but nothing she saw looked good. *Maybe Tracy or Maria will go with me for a pizza,* she thought, heading for the phone. She quickly punched in Tracy's number, then waited. The phone rang ten times at the other end before Caroline finally hung up. She then punched in Maria's number, hoping her friend would be home.

"Maria!" She said with relief when her friend answered the phone.

"Oh hi, Cara." Maria greeted her. "What's going on?"

"Not much. I was just wondering if you'd like to go out and get a pizza with me," Caroline asked.

"Gee, I'd love to, but I can't. It's my grandmother's birthday and we're having a big family get-together in her honor." Maria giggled.

"I never knew I had so many weird relatives!"

"Be sure and wish your grandmother a happy birthday from me," Caroline said with forced brightness.

"Okay." Maria paused for a moment. "Hey Cara, are you all right? You sound sort of depressed."

"Oh no, everything's fine," Caroline replied.

"Are you and Chrissy getting along all right?" Maria asked curiously.

Caroline bit her lip, wishing she could tell Maria how angry she was with Chrissy, but she couldn't. She and Chrissy had decided in the beginning not to tell any of their friends. Drat Chrissy, anyway, this was all her fault.

"Everything's fine between me and Chrissy," she finally answered. "I'll let you get back to your birthday party."

"Well, okay, but I'll call you tomorrow, okay?"

"Okay." Caroline said good-bye, and hung up, more depressed than ever.

I guess I didn't really want pizza after all, she thought to herself, leaving the kitchen and heading back to her bedroom. For a moment she stood in the doorway and stared at her room in dismay. As usual, her side of the room was neat and tidy. Her bed was made up, and her favorite posters neatly lined the wall behind her bed. On her side of the double dresser, her perfume bottles and makeup were all arranged in a special organizer, and she knew exactly where everything was when she needed it. In direct contrast,

Chrissy's side of the bedroom looked like the aftermath of one of her Iowa tornadoes. Chrissy's bed was rumpled, as if she had just thrown on the bedspread and hadn't bothered to pull up the sheets beneath. Thumbtacked haphazardly to the wall behind her bed were stubs of theater tickets, dried-up flowers, a magazine cover, and anything else that had some sort of sentimental value. As for Chrissy's side of the double dresser, it was the picture of utter chaos.

A place for everything and nothing in it's place, Caroline thought.

In the past year and a half of sharing her room with Chrissy, Caroline had gotten used to living with her cousin's messiness. But tonight, it bothered her as if she was seeing it for the first time. *If she is going to be so serious about pretending to be me, why can't she take some of my good traits, like cleaning up after herself,* Caroline thought irritably.

Suddenly, the mess in her room was just too much to take. Caroline stomped across the room and grabbed her box of stationery, then stomped down the hall to the living room. *At least in here I won't be reminded of how she has taken over my life,* Caroline thought as she flopped down in her mother's armchair. Pushing thoughts of her cousin firmly out of her mind, she concentrated on writing a new letter to Luke.

She had just finished her letter when she heard the apartment door open and her parents walk in.

"How was your dinner?" Caroline asked as her parents greeted her.

"Wonderful. We went to that new little Italian place. Your mother got spaghetti with clam sauce and I had the richest, most marvelous lasagne." Richard Kirby patted his stomach with a contented smile. "And with a full stomach, I think I'll go fall asleep in front of the TV. Good night." He smiled at his wife and daughter, then disappeared into his bedroom.

"Did you find something for your supper?" Edith Kirby asked her daughter.

"I wasn't really very hungry earlier, but I think I'll go fix myself a big bowl of granola now," Caroline replied, getting up out of the armchair.

"I'll come with you," Caroline's mom smiled. "I could use a nice, hot cup of tea."

Together they went into the kitchen.

"I assume Chrissy is out with Bart this evening?" Mrs. Kirby said. She filled the kettle with water and placed it on the stove to boil.

"Yeah, they were going to the symphony," Caroline replied, getting the milk out of the refrigerator and setting it on the table.

"That's nice. Bart seems like such a nice boy." Mrs. Kirby sat down at the table and watched as Caroline opened the cereal cabinet.

"The granola is gone!" Caroline said angrily, shaking the empty granola box. "Oh, that's great, that's just great!" She stormed over to the garbage and threw the empty box away, then turned and glared at her mother.

"Why don't you get a bowl of Grapenuts instead?" Caroline's mother suggested.

"Because I don't want Grapenuts! I was all ready for a big bowl of granola and now it's gone!" She flushed slightly, realizing how childish she sounded. But she couldn't help it, this was the last straw! "It's all Chrissy's fault," she continued. "She decided a couple of mornings ago that she was going to start eating granola for breakfast so she could be more like me."

"It sounds like you're pretty angry with Chrissy," Mrs. Kirby observed softly.

"Of course I'm angry with her, she ate all my granola!" Caroline replied, sitting down at the table next to her mother.

"Why do I get the feeling that your anger with Chrissy really has nothing to do with the fact that she ate the last of the granola?" Mrs. Kirby looked at her daughter curiously.

Caroline didn't answer for a moment. "Probably because you're right," she finally admitted. "Oh Mom, I feel like Chrissy is taking over my whole life!" she said in a choked voice.

"Honeybun, I know how difficult it is sometimes, having to share your room and things with Chrissy," her mother began gently.

"That's not it," Caroline replied with a sigh. "It's this thing with Bart, and Chrissy pretending to be me. Chrissy dresses like me, talks like me, she listens to my music and eats all of my favorite foods. I feel like I'm suddenly living with a clone of myself, and I don't like it," Caroline finished unhappily.

"Chrissy does have a tendency to go a little overboard," Caroline's mother agreed. "But honeybun, try to be patient with Chrissy." Mrs. Kirby jumped up as the kettle began to whistle, smiling brightly at her daughter as she poured the boiling water into her teacup. "Besides, haven't you ever heard that imitation is the sincerest form of flattery?"

Caroline gave her mother a weak smile for an answer. She wasn't flattered by Chrissy imitating her. She was mad, and she had a funny feeling that it was going to get much worse before it got better!

Chapter 13

"Caroline, I have got to borrow a pair of your tights and a leotard this morning," Chrissy whispered into Caroline's ear, her voice filled with barely suppressed excitement.

"Chrissy, what time is it?" Caroline demanded, opening her eyes to the semidarkness of the bedroom.

"It's just a few minutes after six o'clock," Chrissy said, not hearing the sharp irritation in Caroline's voice. "I'm really sorry to have to wake you up so early, but I need a pair of your tights and a leotard and I know you don't like me to borrow your things without asking."

"Why do you need my tights and leotard at six o'clock on a Saturday morning?" Caroline asked, not even trying to hide the annoyance in her voice.

Chrissy giggled. Her cousin sure could be grouchy in the morning. "Today is the day I'm supposed to dance for Bart. He isn't coming to pick me up until ten o'clock, but I figured I'd get up early and get some extra practice time." She twirled around in a mini pirouette. "So can I borrow them? I'd really like to borrow the blue striped ones, I know they were your favorites."

"Why not?" Caroline replied sarcastically. "And while you're at it, feel free to take my good pair of ballet shoes. Oh, and don't forget my *Swan Lake* record. You'll probably want to dance to that music."

"Hey, thanks, Caroline!" She gave her cousin a happy hug. "You are really the greatest cousin in the whole wide world!" As she jumped up off the bed and pulled open Caroline's dresser drawer, she heard Caroline flop over to face the wall and heave a loud sigh of aggravation. Chrissy smiled to herself. Caroline was definitely not a morning person!

Chrissy rummaged through the drawer until she found the blue striped leotard and matching tights. Grabbing them, she left the bedroom and headed for the bathroom, excitement coursing through her veins. On this day of all days, there was no way she could have stayed in bed for another second. Today she was going to make her dancing debut!

As she stood beneath the hot spray of the

shower, Chrissy thought back over her past several dates with Bart. On each date they had, she learned more about him, and the more she learned about him, the more she liked him. He was so much more than just a good-looking boy. He had a wonderful sense of humor, and he and Chrissy had shared many laughs—especially when Chrissy managed to make a typically Chrissy Madden foul-up.

She frowned slightly, lathering up her hair with shampoo. She had gotten the impression that Bart's parents were rather stuffy. Oh, Bart hadn't come right out and said his parents were stuffy, but that was the impression she had gotten from things he had said. When she had asked him if he played any sports, he had admitted that although he enjoyed football and basketball, his parents found most organized sports barbaric. Bart had also admitted that he'd never been to a parade or a carnival, and had never visited Santa Claus at a department store when he was young. It amazed Chrissy that Bart could be so rich, yet so deprived at the same time!

As she rinsed her hair, her thoughts turned to the matter at hand—her dancing debut! The excitement once again thundered through her body as she imagined dancing for Bart.

I've got to be crazy, she thought, shutting off the water and stepping out of the shower. *I've got to be totally nuts to think that I can dance for Bart and make him believe I'm Caroline Kirby, the talented ex-dancer.*

But I can do it, her natural optimism protested as she pulled on the tights and leotard. *I've been practicing that easy, little ballet combination that Caroline taught me for weeks. And even if I have to make up a few steps, so long as I look like I know what I am doing, Bart probably won't know the difference.*

Besides, she thought as she fashioned her hair into a demure bun at the nape of her neck, *I just can't put Bart off any longer.*

Each time they had been together, Bart had asked her to dance for him, and each time she had managed to stall him with vague promises. Finally, he had managed to pin her down, telling her that this morning would be perfect. "My dad will be out of town and my mother has a breakfast to attend, so other than the housekeeper and the gardener, we'll have the whole house to ourselves," he'd said. "Cara, please say you will dance for me. I'd really like to see you." His brown eyes had been so soft and pleading that Chrissy had finally relented.

"This is another fine mess you've gotten me into." She grinned at her reflection in the bathroom mirror, pleased by her appearance. Although Caroline's leotard was a bit tight, with her hair pulled back in a bun and her chin lifted haughtily, she looked exactly like a real ballerina! *Now, if I can just manage to dance like a real ballerina,* she thought nervously as she headed for the living room to practice until Bart arrived to pick her up at ten o'clock.

Caroline got up at nine-forty-five and shuffled into the kitchen, where Chrissy was eating a bowl of granola and a stack of french toast.

"Good morning," Chrissy said brightly. "Your mom and dad left a little while ago. They were going down to the market for some fresh fruits and vegetables."

Caroline nodded and poured herself a bowl of granola.

"Well, today's my big day!" Chrissy said excitedly.

"Terrific," Caroline said dryly, going to the refrigerator to get the milk.

"Don't you think I look like a real ballerina?" Chrissy jumped up from the table and twirled around, nearly knocking over her cereal bowl. She froze as the doorbell rang. "Oh, he's here." She looked at Caroline with wide blue eyes. "Aren't you going to wish me luck?" she asked anxiously.

"Good luck," Caroline said with a forced smile.

For a moment Chrissy looked at her cousin curiously, sensing that Caroline was upset with her for something. But as the doorbell rang again, Chrissy dismissed Caroline's ill humor from her mind. *I must be imagining things. Besides, what could she possibly be upset with me about*, she wondered as she opened the front door and smiled brightly at Bart.

Holy Mazoly, Chrissy thought as they pulled up before Bart's home in the Berkeley Hills. Chrissy had expected Bart's house to be nice, but she had not expected the rich grandeur of the mansion before them. *It looks like one of those Southern plantations like in* Gone With the Wind, she thought. Her mouth hung open in awe as she gazed at the huge, two-story colonial home. Six columns extended upward from the sweeping veranda, where Chrissy could easily imagine herself in an old-fashioned dress, sipping mint tulips, or juleps, whatever they were called. She got out of the car, her feet sinking into a carpet of well-tended grass. She was about to follow Bart toward the house, when she heard a loud, piercing shriek from the side of the house. "What—what was that?" she asked, wide-eyed with fear as the shriek sounded again.

"Peacocks," Bart answered with a smile. "My father owns three."

"Of course, peacocks," Chrissy said, as if it was perfectly natural for everyone to own a couple of peacocks.

As she walked with Bart up to the massive front doors, she clutched Caroline's ballet bag and *Swan Lake* record tightly against her chest. Now that she was about to make her debut, her mind was whirling, desperately seeking a way out.

I could always break the Swan Lake *record,* she thought with a sinking sensation as Bart led her into a large foyer with a pink-colored marble floor. *Or I could always pretend to twist my ankle* she thought frantically. *Bart would never make me dance on a twisted ankle.* But, as Bart led her into the large, exquisitely decorated living room and smiled at her in eager anticipation, she knew she couldn't let him down. She would dance for him, and she would dance beautifully!

While he was putting the record on the stereo, Chrissy wandered around the living room. *Bart really lives here* she thought. Somehow, the house didn't suit him. The furniture was spindly and delicate-looking, reminding Chrissy of the kind of furniture she had seen in museums. In fact, the whole room reminded Chrissy of something out of a museum and there was a quiet hush to the house, the same kind of hush one noticed in churches, libraries, and museums. Scattered about the room on several tall, slender pedestals were interesting-looking sculptures, delicate figurines, and different colored, finely etched vases. Chrissy smiled to herself, trying to imagine her brothers living in a place like this. It would be like having three bulls in a china shop!

"There!" Bart turned and faced her as the sound of Tchaikovsky filled the large living room. He sat down on the sofa and looked at her expectantly.

Chrissy smiled at him and swallowed, finding her throat suddenly horribly dry. "Uh . . . do you think I could have something to drink before I begin?" she asked.

"Sure . . . I'll be right back." Bart jumped up off the sofa and disappeared.

When he was gone, Chrissy took several deep breaths. Did Caroline always feel like this before a performance, she wondered—like her throat was stuffed with cotton, and butterflies were doing acrobatics in her stomach? *No wonder she decided not to be a professional ballet dancer,* Chrissy thought.

"I wasn't sure what you wanted, so I brought you a glass of orange juice and a glass of mineral water," Bart said as he came back into the living room carrying two tall glasses.

"Thanks," Chrissy smiled at him gratefully and took the glass of orange juice, drinking it in three quick swallows. Realizing the juice had done nothing to ease the dryness of her throat, she quickly downed the glass of mineral water as well. She knew it was a mistake the minute she finished the glass of water because her stomach gurgled loudly and she felt horribly bloated. *You might as well get this done and over with,* she thought, self-consciously smiling at Bart as she took off the wrap-around skirt she'd worn over her leotard.

Bart sat back down on the sofa, an expectant smile once again on his handsome face. But his smile turned to a look of confusion as Chrissy got into position to begin her dance. "Caroline, aren't you going to put on your ballet shoes?"

"Of course," Chrissy flushed and grabbed Caroline's ballet bag. *Holy cow, here I am trying to act like a real ballerina and I forgot to put on ballet shoes,* she thought, as she quickly slipped on Caroline's pink ballet shoes.

"Don't most ballet dancers warm up a little bit

before actually dancing?" Bart asked her curiously.

"Well . . . sure," Chrissy stammered. She'd often heard Caroline talk about warming up before a class, but Chrissy didn't know exactly what she did to warm up. *Oh well, hopefully Bart doesn't know either.* Quickly she did several deep knee bends, then a series of five jumping jacks, smiling confidently at Bart. *At least look like you know what you're doing,* her brain commanded. She ran in place for a minute or two, then bent down and touched her toes. "There, I think I'm warmed up enough."

"Gosh, I didn't know ballet dancers warmed up like that," Bart exclaimed. "I always thought they did stretching exercises and stuff like that."

Chrissy shrugged. Her confident smile didn't waver, but inside she was all jittery. "All dancers have their own form of warm-up. It's just a matter of personal taste."

Bart nodded as if her explanation made perfect sense.

"Would you mind starting the record over again at the beginning?" Chrissy asked, nervously wiping her sweaty hands down the sides of her too-tight leotard.

"Sure." Bart went over to the stereo and began the *Swan Lake* record from the beginning, then once again sat down on the sofa and smiled at her.

"You realize it has been a long time since I've danced," Chrissy warned him, trying to remember all the things Caroline had told her. Shoulders back, legs turned out, toes pointed, tummy tucked in, bottom tucked under . . . oh, she would never be able to remember everything at the same time!

"Cara, I am not a professional critic," Bart chided softly. "I know it's been a while since you've danced. But I have great confidence in your ability!"

I'm glad one of us has great confidence in me, Chrissy thought as she got into first position. For a moment she simply stood in the ballet position, allowing the music to wash over her, mentally going over in her mind the simple combination of steps Caroline had taught her. Taking a deep breath, Chrissy began to dance.

At first, she was aware that her movements were tense and jerky. Her arms and legs felt like wooden sticks, and she consciously kept her eyes averted from Bart.

But as the steps began to flow more easily, Chrissy felt her movements become smoother, and her confidence began to grow. Her pliés felt deep and controlled, and her turns felt sharp and crisp. *I'm dancing,* she thought in delight, *I'm really dancing!* She began to improvise steps, making her arm movements bigger and more dramatic. Chrissy forgot all about Bart's presence in the room, and totally gave herself up to the stirring sound of the music and the pleasure of her dancing. *I feel like a real ballerina,* she thought, lifting her chin in the air as she had seen Coppelia do on that fateful blind date.

Neither Chrissy nor Bart saw Bart's mother come into the house and pause in the doorway of the living room.

"What is going on here?" Mrs. Reed demanded.

The sharp, indignant voice caused Chrissy to stumble in the middle of a turn. Her arms flew out in surprise, causing her fingertips to accidently brush against one of the tall, slender pedestals upon which sat an exquisite, antique-looking vase.

Chrissy froze in horror as the pedestal rocked forward just enough for the vase to slide off. As if in slow motion, the beautiful vase turned top over bottom and crashed to the floor, where it shattered into hundreds of pieces.

Chapter 14

"My vase!" Mrs. Reed stared at the shattered vase in disbelief, then looked at her son, her features set rigidly. "Bart, I would like to speak with you for a moment . . . alone," she said tensely, not even looking in Chrissy's direction.

"I'll . . . I'll just wait out in the hallway," Chrissy mumbled miserably, slowly backing out of the living room. "Bart . . . Mrs. Reed . . ." She looked beseechingly at both of them. "I am really sorry about the vase . . ."

Mrs. Reed gasped in horror as Chrissy backed into another pedestal, this one holding a plaster sculpture.

Just in time Chrissy turned and grabbed the pedestal with one hand and the sculpture with the other, steadying them until they were stable.

Then she ran out of the living room and into the hallway without looking back. Once in the hallway, she stared at the pink-marbled floor, biting down hard on her bottom lip to stop her tears from falling. She had blown it for sure this time. Bart would never want to speak to her again! She cringed as she thought about the shattered vase. She hoped it hadn't been one of those Ting, or Ming, or whatever they were vases. She bit her lip again as she remembered the look on Mrs. Reed's face. Mrs. Reed hadn't looked anything like the smiling picture that Chrissy had seen in the newspaper. She had looked really, really mad, and all her attractive features had been pulled tightly with her anger.

Chrissy traced a white line in the marble floor with the toe of Caroline's ballet slipper, wondering what Bart's mother was saying to him. She followed the vein as it led across the floor to one side of the living room doorway.

As Chrissy reached the end, she stopped abruptly. Voices filtered out from the living room. *I really shouldn't do this*, she thought, taking a step closer to the open doorway. *But I'm not really eavesdropping*, she assured herself. *Eavesdropping is when you put a drinking glass against a wall to hear what's happening in the next room, or when you stand in an alley beneath a partially closed window and listen to a private conversation. But Bart and his mother know I am here in the hall, and they left the living room doors open anyway, so this really isn't eavesdrop-*

ping at all, she decided as she listened closely to the conversation going on in the next room.

". . . . that girl didn't have the talent to be a professional ballet dancer and that is why she quit," Mrs. Reed was saying.

"Mother, her name is Caroline Kirby," Bart said patiently. "And it has been quite a while since she has done any dancing at all. It isn't fair for you to make a judgment about her talent based on the brief amount of time you saw her dancing."

Chrissy's heart expanded at the sound of Bart's defending her.

"Bart, I know what I saw, and that girl is no dancer," Mrs. Reed continued firmly. She made a small, disgusted noise. "And my vase, she broke one of my favorite vases." Chrissy heard a rustling noise, then the tinkling of porcelain pieces being picked up.

"Mother, it was an accident." Bart stressed the last word of his sentence. "You startled both of us when you came in."

"Accident or not, it's obvious that girl has no real breeding. Where does she go to school?"

"Maxwell High," Bart answered in a low voice that Chrissy could just barely hear.

"Maxwell High School!" Mrs. Reed's voice rose indignantly. "Bart dear, that's a public school. It's no wonder she's so poorly behaved."

Chrissy frowned as she heard this. Breaking the vase had been an accident—that didn't mean she was poorly behaved. Besides, what was wrong with public schools? *I bet Mrs. Reed would really have a hairy canary if she knew about Danbury High*, Chrissy thought, recalling the loud, boisterous atmosphere of her school back in Iowa.

"Mother, honestly, what difference does it make where she goes to school? She is really a very nice girl," Bart insisted, much to Chrissy's delight.

"Bart, darling, this Kirby girl is simply not your type. I would think that would be obvious by her actions here today," Mrs. Reed continued sternly. "The girl is apparently very clumsy, and has demonstrated an extreme disregard for my possessions. I know her mother, and she is nothing but an ordinary store clerk!"

Anger, swift and hot rose in Chrissy at Mrs. Reed's last remark. *Why that old biddy*, she thought angrily. *How dare she look down her snooty nose at my Aunt Edith! Aunt Edith is the best aunt in the whole wide world!* She almost stormed into the living room to confront Bart's mother, but then she stopped herself. *If I go in there to defend Aunt Edith, Mrs. Reed will know that I was listening to their conversation, and that will only prove to her that everything she said about me is true*, Chrissy thought miserably. *Besides, I don't want to embarrass Bart any more than I already have in front of his mother.*

"Mother, Mrs. Kirby isn't a store clerk, she manages the art gallery," Bart explained, his voice sounding troubled and confused.

Mrs. Reed heaved a loud, exasperated sigh. "Bart, I really think it would be best for everyone if you would take her home now and not see her anymore. After all, there are plenty of lovely girls with a similar background to yours who would be much more suitable." There was a note of finality to Mrs. Reed's words, and knowing the conversation was drawing to an end, Chrissy quickly moved away from the doorway.

She was standing by the front door when Bart came out of the living room carrying her ballet bag and the *Swan Lake* record. "I'm sorry you had to wait so long," he said, handing her the bag and the record.

"That's all right," Chrissy said softly. "Bart . . . I am really, really sorry about your mother's vase." She looked up at him through eyes that were blurry with unshed tears.

"It wasn't your fault," Bart tried to assure her. "I shouldn't have had you dance for me in the living room." He smiled at her, but his smile seemed distant, not the same warm smile that Chrissy had grown to love, and she felt her heart sink down to her toes. "Come on, I'll drive you home," he said, and together they walked out of the Reed house and got into Bart's car.

For most of the drive back to the Kirby apartment, both Bart and Chrissy were silent. *I wish he would say something,* she thought. *He must be thinking about what his mother said. But surely Bart doesn't agree with her. Does he?* Chrissy wanted to defend herself from all the things his mother had said about her, but she didn't want him to know that she had heard the entire conversation from outside the doorway. And so, the atmosphere in the car felt heavy with silence—but not as heavy as Chrissy's heart.

It's over between us, she thought sadly, looking out the car window and swiping at a tear that made it's way down her cheek. *Rats, rats, double rats! Why couldn't one of San Francisco's famous earthquakes have struck at the exact moment that I knocked over that stupid pedestal,* she thought. *Then Bart and his mother would have blamed the earthquake.*

She looked over at Bart, noticing the troubled expression on his face. "Bart . . . about the vase, I'll be glad to pay for it," she offered, knowing it was a pretty ridiculous thing to say. She could give Mrs. Reed her weekly allowance every week for the rest of her life and it probably wouldn't even cover the sales tax on such an expensive vase. Still, she felt she had to offer, just to prove to Bart that she didn't have a total disregard for other people's possessions.

"Forget it, Caroline," he said without looking at her, the confused expression still on his face. "Really, don't worry about it." This time he turned and smiled at her, but it was not the warm, understanding smile she wanted to see from him.

She looked back out the window and sighed. She would have liked to ask him to pull the car over so she could look him in the eye and tell him she was not like what his mother had said. She wanted to demand an answer as to why it mattered where she went to school. She wanted to know why it mattered that Aunt Edith did an honest day's work for a living. And perhaps the old Chrissy would have done just that, but in the past couple of weeks, in her role as Caroline Kirby, Chrissy had learned some of her cousin's self-control. She realized that in being her impulsive self, she would only show him that she had "no real breeding" as Mrs. Reed had put it.

Chrissy sighed miserably as Bart parked his car at the curb in front of the Kirby's apartment house.

"You don't have to walk me up to the door," she said, wanting only to hurry up and get away from him before she really started to cry.

"I'll call you," Bart told her, but Chrissy realized that he was just being polite and didn't really mean it. With a mumbled good-bye, she escaped from the car and ran up the steps to the front door. When she reached the top step, she turned and looked back in time to see Bart drive off. A sob caught in her throat, and she knew she would probably never see him again.

I should have known it would never work out if I pretended to be somebody I wasn't, she admonished herself. *Bart and I couldn't have gone on forever, not when our whole relationship was based on a lie.*

With a strangled cry of despair, she turned and stumbled into the house.

"Chrissy, what's wrong?" Caroline looked up

from the television when she heard Chrissy's heart-wrenching sobs.

"Oh Cara, it was a complete disaster, a real catastrophe!" Chrissy bit her bottom lip to still her sobs and sat down next to Caroline on the sofa.

"What happened, Chrissy?" Caroline asked anxiously. No matter how angry she became with Chrissy, Caroline never liked to see her cousin cry.

"It was so horrible," Chrissy wailed and broke into loud, gulping sobs. "I was dancing . . . and . . . Bart . . . and his mother . . . and the vase . . . crash!" She wailed again.

"Chrissy, slow down, I can't understand you," Caroline said, wishing her cousin would stop the deep shudders that wracked her body. "Now, tell me what happened again, only this time more slowly."

It took several minutes for Caroline to pry the whole story out of the still sobbing Chrissy, but finally she managed to get a pretty clear picture of what had happened.

"Bart's mother certainly doesn't sound very nice," Caroline remarked when Chrissy had finished her story.

Chrissy sniffled loudly and swiped at her wet face with the back of her hand. "She's not! She's a snob. A real snooty, patooty."

Caroline swallowed a giggle at Chrissy's expression. Chrissy caught the fleeting look of amusement on her cousin's face and answered with a small grin of her own. But the grin soon faded. "Oh, Cara, I liked Bart so much."

"Are you sure it's really over between the two of you? I mean, did he actually tell you it was all over?" Caroline asked.

"No." Chrissy recalled Bart's distant smile. "He didn't actually come right out and tell me, but I could tell by the way he acted when he brought me home."

"I'm really sorry, Chrissy." Caroline said softly. And she was truly very sorry, but she was also grateful that now things could go back to normal. Chrissy would go back to being Chrissy Madden—wear her own clothes, eat her own foods and, most important, stop dancing around the apartment. Caroline would have her own life back again.

Chrissy shrugged. "Deep down in my heart, I knew it would never last between Bart and me. But, you know," she continued thoughtfully, "one good thing has come out of all of this."

"What's that?" Caroline asked curiously.

"Well, right before Bart's mother came in, it was really strange. When I first started to dance for Bart, it didn't go very well. I was all stiff and nervous, and really pretty terrible." Chrissy's face took on a dreamy expression. "Then suddenly, I began to really feel the music, and I forgot all about Bart being in the room. All that seemed important was that I was dancing!" She looked at Caroline with excitement radiating from her bright blue eyes. "Holy Mazoly, Cara, all this time I didn't realize it, but I really believe I was born to be a ballet dancer!"

"Holy Mazoly," Caroline echoed with a weak, forced smile.

Chapter 15

"Caroline, don't you have any purple leotards?"
Chrissy's voice floated across the bedroom as she
rummaged through Caroline's dresser drawer. "I
really like purple, and I think a purple leotard
would look nice on me. Why do you have so
many blue ones?"

"Chrissy, it's hardly morning. I don't know why
you've set your alarm so early the past three
mornings," Caroline grumbled, turning over and
burying her head beneath her pillow.

"You know I need the extra time to practice my
ballet," Chrissy explained, accidentally slamming
Caroline's drawer with a bang. "I guess I'll have
to wear blue," she sighed, heading for the bathroom with one of Caroline's leotards in her hand.

Once she was gone, Caroline rolled over on her

back and frowned up at the ceiling. She was sick of Chrissy's bubbling enthusiasm for her new career choice. Caroline shared everything with Chrissy except ballet—that was the one thing that had always been hers alone.

"And now Chrissy's taking that over, too." Caroline muttered as she slipped back to sleep until her own alarm woke her again.

After school that afternoon, Caroline decided to prove to herself that she was still the dancer in the family, not Chrissy. For once, Chrissy was busy studying in the bedroom for an American History test, her mother was still at the gallery, and her father had his work spread out on the dining room table so that Caroline could have the living room all to herself.

She sat down in the middle of the floor and spread her legs out in a straddle position, then she reached out and touched the toes of her left foot, pulling and stretching muscles that hadn't been exercised in a long time. Just warming up made her feel better. Every time she saw Chrissy in her too-tight leotard, leaping and jumping about, Caroline remembered what she had given up when she had quit ballet. The more Caroline saw Chrissy try to dance, the more compelled she felt to show her cousin how to do it properly. She hated watching Chrissy butcher beautiful ballet steps. Although Caroline had to admit, what Chrissy lacked in basic training and natural aptitude, she more than made up for in enthusiasm.

Caroline stood up and began to do a series of pliés, feeling a sense of satisfaction as she saw the graceful curve of her arms in front of her, felt her legs automatically seeking the proper ballet positions. It felt wonderful to do something and know she did it well. She'd almost forgotten the joy and freedom she experienced whenever she danced.

Caroline didn't need any music to dance to, the music was in her head, in the memory of all her years of training. She closed her eyes and moved gracefully to the orchestra playing in her mind.

She was only vaguely aware of the doorbell ringing, but continued what she was doing when she heard her father answer the door. She did a quick ballet turn, stumbling as she opened her eyes and saw Bart Reed enter the living room. "Bart!" Her voice squeaked out in astonishment.

"Hi Chrissy, your uncle let me in." Bart's face held a strange expression as he looked at her.

"Oh . . ." Caroline smiled at him self-consciously. "Uh . . . have a seat and I'll just go get Caroline." But as she turned to leave the room, Chrissy came bounding into the living room, stopping in surprise when she saw Bart and Caroline. It took her exactly one second to grasp the situation.

"Chrissy, have you been practicing those ballet steps I taught you?" Chrissy asked Caroline, her bright blue eyes silently pleading with Caroline not to give away their secret. Chrissy smiled at Bart. "Chrissy has decided she wants to learn a little ballet, so I've been giving her lessons," she explained. "Of course, I'm just teaching her very simple things, but I'm really proud of her progress."

She's talking about me like I'm some kind of idiot, Caroline thought resentfully. "I think I'll go change," she mumbled, leaving Chrissy and Bart alone in the living room.

After she left, there was a moment of uncomfortable silence between Chrissy and Bart, and when they did finally speak, they both spoke at the same time.

"I thought you were going to call me..." Chrissy began.

"I've been meaning to call you..." Bart said.

They both broke off and laughed. "You first," Chrissy said, happy to see that his smile was just as warm and wonderful as ever.

"I started to say that I've been meaning to call you but it's midterm week at school and I've really been bogged down with homework." He looked at his watch. "In fact, I really can't stay now. I just stopped by to see if you'd like to go with me to see *Giselle* next Saturday night. The New York City Ballet is on tour."

Chrissy's heart fluttered, and she had a crazy desire to wrap him in a big bear hug, she was so happy. So they hadn't broken up after all!

"I'd love to go with you," she answered, keeping her voice calm.

"Great, I'll pick you up at seven-fifteen." He turned to leave.

"Bart?" She wanted to ask him about his

mother. Had Mrs. Reed taken back all the things she'd said, or had Bart chosen to ignore them?

"Yes?" He paused and looked at her.

"Oh, never mind." *He asked you out again, didn't he?* she thought. *That's all that matters.* "I'll see you Saturday night," she said, smiling brightly.

"Sure. See you then," Bart replied, then he was gone.

"Yahoo!" Chrissy yelled.

"I guess that yell means that things are all right between you and Bart," Caroline said dryly as she reappeared in the living room clad in jeans and a blouse.

"Everything is wonderful, stupendous, perfect between me and Bart!" Chrissy exclaimed, causing Caroline to wince as she did a clumsy jeté across the room. "I guess it doesn't matter that his mother thinks I'm not the right type for him." She did three quick ballet turns across the floor, then paused, swaying dizzily. "He came by to ask me out for Saturday night!" She leapt across the room, landing with all the grace of a baby elephant.

"Chrissy, would you stop that!" Caroline snapped sharply, unable to stand another second of watching Chrissy's awkward movements. "Where are you and Bart going on Saturday night?" she asked as Chrissy flopped down in one of the large armchairs.

"To see the New York City Ballet do *Giselle*," Chrissy answered.

A wave of resentment swept over Caroline. "How nice," she said tightly and stood up. "I just remembered, I have some homework to do." Without another word to Chrissy, she headed down the hall to the bedroom and shut the door.

It isn't fair. It should be me going to the ballet, not Chrissy, she thought. *Chrissy Madden doesn't give a darn about the ballet, she's just going through another one of her stupid phases!* Caroline threw herself on her bed and pounded her pillow in frustration. *It's just not fair!*

Caroline and Chrissy were both in the bedroom later that evening when the telephone rang.

"I'll get it." Chrissy jumped up off the bed, glad for any diversion that would take her away from her school books.

Caroline barely looked up from her letter as her cousin flew out of the bedroom to answer the phone. With Chrissy so excited about her date with Bart on Saturday night, Caroline was once again aware of her own loneliness. Iowa was so far away from San Francisco and Luke was so far away from her. She could only hope that she and Luke would both get accepted to Colorado University, then nothing could keep them apart.

She was nibbling on the end of her pencil, trying to think of something else to write when Chrissy came back into the bedroom, a stricken expression on her face.

"Chrissy, what's wrong? Who was on the phone?" Caroline asked anxiously. Her first thought was that Chrissy had gotten some bad news from home.

"Bart—it was Bart on the phone," Chrissy answered in a small choked voice. "He called to tell me to forget our date for Saturday night. He doesn't ever want to see me again." Chrissy looked at Caroline with watery blue eyes and burst into loud sobs.

Chapter 16

Caroline walked slowly along the sidewalk, enjoying the feel of the warm spring sunshine on her shoulders. Chrissy had ridden home from school with some of their friends, but Caroline had decided that she needed some time alone—especially away from her cousin.

I wish today wasn't Friday, she thought. Like most people, Caroline usually looked forward to Friday, but now she dreaded a full weekend spent with Chrissy. Since Bart had called two nights earlier to break up, Chrissy had alternated between sessions of frantic ballet dancing and moping around with an utterly miserable expression on her face. If there was one thing worse than Chrissy's exhausting high spirits, it was her melancholy moods.

Caroline shifted her school books from one arm to the other and sighed, remembering the conversation she'd had with her cousin only that morning.

"I've been doing a lot of thinking about college," Chrissy had said as the two girls sat in the kitchen eating breakfast.

"What about it?" Caroline had asked curiously.

"I've decided to write a letter to Colorado University and find out what kinds of scholarships they have to offer. I know you won't have any problem getting in, but even though I worked hard on the application I'm not so sure that they'll accept me." She looked at Caroline glumly. "The way I'm feeling right now, I just can't bear the thought of us going off to different colleges." Chrissy looked at Caroline as if she was her last friend on earth.

Caroline hadn't said anything, but inside she was appalled by the whole idea of Chrissy and she spending the next four years together at the same college.

I want my own life, Caroline now thought as she paused to peer into the window of a dress boutique. She didn't want to share four more years with an inconsiderate, harebrained cousin! *Darn it, I'm really looking forward to being completely independent in college. Independent from everyone—including Chrissy.* She frowned and moved away from the boutique window, heading uphill toward home.

"Caroline!"

The voice calling her name came from the sports car that pulled up along the curb beside her. She bent down to look at the driver and was shocked to see Bart Reed. "Can I talk to you for a minute, Caroline?" he asked.

"Okay," she agreed, wondering what he wanted to talk to her about. Then it struck her. *He hadn't called her Chrissy—he'd called her Caroline.* Somehow, he had found out the truth.

"Hop in," he said, reaching across to open the passenger door. "I'm glad I found you."

Caroline got in the car, a flush of color staining her cheeks. "When did you find out?" she asked softly.

"Wednesday night," Bart answered, not looking at her but instead looking at his hands resting on the steering wheel of the car.

Caroline nodded, not surprised to find out that he'd discovered the truth on the night he'd called to break up with Chrissy. "How did you find out?" she asked curiously.

"Several times when I was out with Caro . . . Chrissy," he corrected himself, clutching the wheel tightly in two fists, "she would do something or say something that just didn't go along with what Madeleine had told me about Caroline Kirby. Then when I walked in the other night and saw you dancing," he sighed heavily. "Even though I just saw you dancing for a minute, it was long enough for me to realize that you weren't some farm girl practicing steps you'd just learned." He studied his hands with a frown.

"After I left your apartment, I went over to Maddie's house. She had the program from last year's ballet performance, and it had your picture in it." For the first time since she had gotten into his car, he turned and looked at her, a spark of anger lighting his brown eyes. "It was a pretty crummy thing you and your cousin did."

Caroline flushed and looked away from him with embarrassment. "We didn't mean for it to turn out this way. We just sort of figured you and Chrissy would go out one time and that would be the end of it." She flushed again and shifted her books in her arms. "For what it's worth, Bart, I'm sorry."

"Are you?" He turned and looked at her, a thoughtful expression on his face. "The way I see it, you owe me a date."

Caroline looked up at him with surprise.

"Look, Caroline, I've got two great tickets for the ballet tomorrow night. I bought them so that I could take Caroline Kirby to the ballet. Will Caroline Kirby go with me?" he paused a moment. "The real Caroline Kirby?"

Her first impulse was to turn him down flat. After all, she had Luke, and Bart did dump Chrissy. "Bart, I really don't think . . ." she began.

"Caroline, you owe me one." Bart's voice was low and insistent.

Caroline felt a small tinge of guilt. This whole mess *was* all her fault. If she had just said no to Madeleine from the very beginning, then none of this would have happened. Beneath the guilt, she also felt a sense of longing. She would love to see *Giselle. And why shouldn't I?* she thought hesitantly. *Why shouldn't I go with Bart tomorrow night?* After all, Bart was right, she owed him a date. Besides, she had already given up an opportunity to see one ballet, she didn't want to pass up another!

"All right, I'll go with you," she answered softly, fighting back the guilt she felt at thoughts of Chrissy.

"Okay, I'll pick you up at seven-fifteen tomorrow night." Bart smiled, but it was a smile that just curved his lips—it didn't touch his eyes.

"Okay, I'll see you tomorrow night." Caroline got out of the car and waved as Bart drove off. The smile on her face faltered as she thought once again of Chrissy. *Surely Chrissy will understand,* she consoled herself, continuing her uphill walk. *If Bart wants a date with the real Caroline Kirby, I can't exactly say no after everything that's happened.*

Caroline lifted her chin in determination. *Besides, I shouldn't feel bad, not after the way Chrissy has been such a gigantic pain lately. I'll just go home and explain to her how Bart asked me to the ballet and I accepted. No big deal!*

"Hello?" she called out as she stepped in through the front door, ready to face Chrissy and tell her about the date with Bart.

"In here," Chrissy's voice called from the living room.

Caroline went into the living room and found

Chrissy sitting on the sofa, her face red and tear-stained.

"I didn't know whether you would be home yet or not," Caroline said, sitting down on the sofa next to her cousin.

"I'm home." Chrissy sighed miserably. "The rest of the kids were going to get a pizza, but I told them just to bring me on home. How can I think of pizza when I have a broken heart?" She turned misery-filled eyes to Caroline. "Oh, Cara, I can't stop thinking about Bart."

Caroline didn't say anything, knowing now that there was no way she could tell Chrissy about her date with Bart. Chrissy would never understand.

Chrissy looked at Caroline with a small, sad smile. "We make quite a pair. You're lonely because the guy you like lives thousands of miles away, and I'm lonely because I messed everything up with the guy I really like." She sighed heavily. "Why don't we plan on doing something tomorrow to pick up our spirits. We could go shopping all day, then maybe go to a movie, and top it off with a Cable Car Special at Mama's Ice Cream."

"Why don't we go to Mama's this evening?" Caroline suggested cautiously.

"No, I just don't feel like going tonight. I'm just not in the mood and besides, I've got to practice my ballet." She looked at Caroline curiously. "Why won't you go with me tomorrow night?"

"Who knows what I'll be doing tomorrow night?" Caroline got up from the sofa, a guilty flush on her face. "I mean, I don't know what my plans are yet." She kept her eyes averted from Chrissy's. "Why don't you see if Justine or Tracy or Maria will go with you?" She turned to leave the room. "I'm going to go change my clothes."

Chrissy watched Caroline leave the room, a thoughtful expression on her face. *What's wrong with Caroline?* she wondered, as she got up from the sofa and followed her cousin into the bedroom.

"So, what are you going to do if you don't go with me tomorrow night?" Chrissy asked, flopping on her bed.

"How should I know?" Caroline snapped defensively. "Is it necessary for me to check out my daily itinerary with you?" she asked, her guilt making her voice sharp and tense.

"Excuse moi," Chrissy exclaimed sarcastically. "What has your feathers all ruffled?"

"You have!" Caroline exploded, eyeing her cousin resentfully. "Honestly Chrissy, lately you've been driving me crazy!"

Chrissy looked at her cousin in surprise. "What have *I* done?" she asked.

"What have you done?" Caroline eyed Chrissy bitterly. "You've taken over my whole life, that's what you've done!"

"What are you talking about?"

"I'm talking about this," Caroline walked over to the pile of dirty clothes on the floor. She bent over and picked out a pair of her slacks and two of her best sweaters. "You're wearing all my clothes." She dropped the clothes back on the floor. "And that's not all, you're eating all my favorite foods, you're doing all the things I like to do. You've even taken over my ballet dancing!" Tears of frustration glistened in Caroline's eyes. "I just can't wait until I leave this house for college. Maybe then I won't have to share everything with you!" Caroline clapped her hand over her mouth. She hadn't meant to be quite so spiteful.

"I had no idea it was such a burden for you to share things with me," Chrissy said, her voice thick with emotion. "And as I recall, it was all your idea for me to pretend to be you in the first place!"

"Yes, but it wasn't my idea for you to go overboard," Caroline replied tightly.

Chrissy got off the bed. "Well, I certainly won't do anything more to overwhelm you. As far as I'm concerned, from now on we share the same bedroom, and nothing else." Then she turned and left the room.

Caroline felt a sickness in the pit of her stomach as she watched Chrissy disappear into the hallway. She hated to fight, especially with Chrissy. *Maybe it's best that I told Chrissy what's been bothering me,* Caroline consoled herself. But her thoughts didn't make her feel any better.

As the evening progressed, Caroline only managed to feel worse and worse. During dinner, neither of them spoke a word to the other. And although they both sat in the living room watching a movie on television that night, they might just as well have been miles apart.

Well, at least I don't have to worry about feeling overwhelmed anymore, Caroline thought as she got into bed that night. *Now, instead of feeling overwhelmed by Chrissy, I just feel lonely and empty and sad.* She turned to face the wall as she heard Chrissy come into the bedroom and get into bed. She just hoped Chrissy wouldn't find out about her date with Bart. *Things are chilly now, but if Chrissy finds out I'm going to the ballet with Bart tomorrow night, things won't be just chilly, they'll be positively arctic!* With a shiver of unhappiness, Caroline closed her eyes and slowly fell asleep.

Chapter 17

Fortunately for Caroline, Chrissy left early the following evening to meet Tracy at Mama's Ice Cream Store. As soon as she heard her cousin leave, Caroline rushed to get ready for her date with Bart Reed.

As she fastened the pearls around her neck, she couldn't help but remember the fun she'd had getting Chrissy ready for her first date with Bart. In fact, all day Caroline had been thinking about how much fun and laughter Chrissy had brought into her life. She honestly couldn't imagine life without her crazy cousin anymore.

The sound of the doorbell startled Caroline out of her daydreams. This date is a big mistake, she thought glumly as she opened the front door.

Bart stood at the door, looking extremely

uncomfortable. "Hi, Caroline," he said, smiling nervously.

"Hi, Bart," she replied. "Don't worry, Chrissy isn't home." She immediately noticed Bart become more relaxed.

"Well, are you ready?" he asked.

She nodded, feeling a tinge of irritation. If he hadn't wanted to be here, then why had he persuaded her to go out with him?

They were both silent as they got into his car and headed toward the Civic Center.

"Are you good friends with Madeleine Walsh?" Caroline asked, attempting to break the uncomfortable silence.

"Not really. I've spoken to her a few times at the country club, and I stopped by her house the other day, like I told you." Bart looked at her sideways. "Did she know about this switch with you and Chrissy? She acted awfully innocent when I asked to see your picture in the ballet program."

"No, she didn't know. Nobody knew except Chrissy and me, and of course my parents," Caroline explained.

Once again they fell silent. *I wish I wasn't here,* Caroline thought to herself miserably. *I wish it was Luke taking me to the ballet.*

"I was really pleased that I was able to get such good seats for tonight," Bart said, easing his car around a corner. "They're first row balcony seats. I think you get a real good overall view from the balcony."

"Personally, I prefer the orchestra level. I like to see the dancers up close," Caroline replied. She knew she sounded perverse, but she didn't care. The whole date was a big mistake, and she felt that in being here with Bart, she was betraying the two people she loved most—Luke and Chrissy.

"I'm sorry, I guess you'll just have to slum it tonight in the balcony," Bart said with a touch of sarcasm.

"I'll do my best," Caroline returned, grateful that they had arrived at the auditorium.

It wasn't until they were seated in their balcony seats that they once again attempted conversation.

"I've always found the story of *Giselle* to be very romantic," Bart said softly.

Caroline frowned thoughtfully. "I've always thought of *Giselle* as tragic. I mean, Giselle *does* die."

"Well, yes, but even in death she tries to save the life of the man she loves," Bart protested. That's tragic, but it's also romantic."

"I don't find that romantic, I think it's foolish," Caroline exclaimed firmly. "After all, the man she loved had betrayed her."

Bart opened his mouth as if to argue with her, but instead clamped his lips closed with a frown.

Caroline glanced over at him, and immediately regretted that she'd been so disagreeable. "*Giselle* is supposed to be one of the most demanding roles for a dancer," Caroline remarked in a lighter tone of voice.

"Obviously I don't have your expertise in that area," Bart replied, and Caroline heard him breathe a deep sigh of relief as the lights dimmed and the orchestra began to play.

As the first act unfolded, Caroline and Bart sat quietly, fascinated by the magnificent ballet. But while Caroline was enjoying the action on the stage, her mind was whirling with other thoughts.

She had a feeling that Bart didn't want to be with her any more than she wanted to be with him, and for some reason that made her very angry. Why had he invited her to come with him in the first place? He certainly wasn't going out of his way to be charming or attentive—not that she cared anyway!

During the first half of the ballet, Caroline often felt Bart's gaze on her, as if he were studying her. *He's making me feel like some sort of insect beneath a microscope*, she thought. Thankfully, Bart went to get them a drink almost as soon as the lights rose for intermission. If Caroline hadn't wanted to see the rest of the ballet, she would have asked Bart to take her home right then. *This whole date has been a huge mistake*, she thought for the umpteenth time that night. *The only guy I want to be with is Luke.* Caroline smiled tightly as Bart returned with two sodas.

"Isn't the girl who's playing Giselle wonderful?" Bart whispered as the second act began.

Caroline hesitated for a moment. Should she agree with him just to avoid more tension, or should she tell the truth? She honestly didn't think the dancer's movements were as sharp and crisp as they should be. "Actually, I've been sort of disappointed in her," she replied at last.

"You're kidding!" Bart looked at her in amazement, lowering his voice as the people in front of them turned around to give them a disapproving glance.

"You're kidding," he repeated in a hushed whisper. "I think she's great. And she's so pretty too—just like Giselle."

"How typically chauvinistic," Caroline scoffed. "Just because she's pretty, you automatically assume she's talented!"

"I don't think that!" Bart protested heatedly, causing the people in front of them to turn and shush them. Caroline's cheeks burned with embarrassment. "I'm perfectly capable of separating physical beauty and talent!" He glared at her. "Maybe you're just jealous because you don't dance anymore!"

"That's the most ridiculous thing I've ever heard!" This time it was Caroline's angry voice that made people turn and look at them. *Mon Dieu*, she thought in embarrassment, *we're causing an awful scene.* She wanted to argue the point with him further, but she couldn't bear the thought of people staring at her, so she clamped her mouth shut. For the rest of the ballet,

Caroline and Bart sat stiffly, neither even daring to look at the other.

When the last curtain call was over, they walked silently back to the car. "Would you like to go some place and get something to eat?" Bart asked politely as he switched on the engine.

"No thank you, I'd really rather just go on home," Caroline replied softly.

Bart nodded, looking as relieved as Caroline felt. But when they pulled up in front of the Kirby apartment house, Caroline turned to him at the same time he turned to her.

"Bart, I'm sorry that . . ." Caroline began.

"Caroline, I apologize for . . ." Bart said.

They smiled shyly at each other. "Go ahead," Bart prompted.

"Well, I want to apologize for this whole evening." Caroline gave him a small, apologetic smile. "It's been a dismal failure, hasn't it?" Bart nodded, but kept his gaze directed out the window. "I should never have agreed to go out with you," Caroline continued. "You see, I've already got a boyfriend, who lives in Iowa. That's why Chrissy agreed to go out with you in my place." She looked at Bart thoughtfully. "I never gave you a chance tonight. All I could think about was Luke, and how I wished he was with me instead of you. I'm sorry, that wasn't very fair to you." Her cheeks flushed lightly.

"That's all right." Bart turned toward her and for the first time all evening, he smiled so that it lit up his whole face. "All evening I've been thinking about Chrissy and how I wanted to be with her."

Caroline laughed softly. "Well, it looks like we've both learned a lesson tonight."

Bart grinned at Caroline. "Your cousin is really a very special girl."

"Yes, she is." Caroline agreed, realizing how true it was. Oh sure, Chrissy could be impulsive and careless, and a pain in the derriére, but her good points made her bad points seem unimportant. Caroline frowned suddenly. "Bart, Chrissy doesn't know that I went out with you tonight." She looked at Bart worriedly. "She'll be furious when she finds out."

"I'll explain everything to her," Bart said thoughtfully. "In fact, I'd like to come in right now and talk to her. I have some apologizing to do."

So do I, Caroline thought, remembering all the hateful things she'd said to Chrissy the night before. "Come on, let's go inside and tell Chrissy what fools we've been." Caroline smiled at Bart, and together they climbed out of the car and headed up the stairs to the Kirby apartment.

Chapter 18

Chrissy sat on the sofa in her bathrobe, eating a candy bar and feeling utterly miserable. Even the Cable Car Special she'd had earlier in the evening at Mama's hadn't pulled her out of the pits of depression.

She popped the last of the chocolate into her mouth and licked her fingers. *I'll probably wake up with a face full of zits from eating all this chocolate*, she thought, then sighed. What did it matter if her face broke out? Who would care if she looked like the 'before' picture in an ad for acne medication?

Oh Bart, don't you miss me as much as I miss you? We had so much fun together, she thought wistfully.

The last couple of days had been the most miserable Chrissy had ever known. First the breakup with Bart, then the fight with Caroline. She frowned at the thought of her cousin. *Where on earth did Cara go tonight*, she wondered. *And why wouldn't she tell me?*

Chrissy had been doing a lot of thinking about the things Caroline had said to her the night before, and she wasn't mad anymore. If she put herself in Caroline's shoes, she could see how she might have been a pest. She jumped up as she heard the front door opening. *Maybe that's Cara now,* she thought, hurrying to the door. But before she'd taken even two steps into the hallway, Chrissy froze. At the other end of the hall stood Caroline—with Bart right beside her! A sense of betrayal swept over Chrissy, and she trembled with rage as she stared at the pair.

"Chrissy . . ." Caroline stepped toward her cousin.

"Caroline, could I talk to Chrissy alone?" Bart asked softly.

Caroline nodded, and with one last pleading look at Chrissy, she disappeared into the bedroom, leaving Bart and Chrissy alone.

"I really don't see what we have to talk about," Chrissy said tightly, pulling her robe around her self-consciously.

"We have a lot to talk about," Bart replied, gently taking Chrissy's arm and guiding her to the sofa in the living room.

Chrissy was numb with hurt. She knew Caroline had been really angry with her the night before, but she hadn't realized what a traitor her cousin could be! To go out with Bart! She looked down at her hands folded in her lap, pressing back hot tears of pain.

"I took Caroline to the ballet tonight," Bart began.

"Gee, I hope the two of you had a marvelous time," Chrissy said bitterly, unable to even look at Bart.

"Actually, we had a horrible time. All Caroline could think about was Luke, and all I could think about was you." Bart smiled as she looked up at him in surprise. "The night I broke up with you, I had just found out that you weren't the real Caroline Kirby, and I was so angry! I thought that you and Caroline were having a lot of laughs at my expense."

"It wasn't anything like that," Chrissy protested.

"Now I know that, but I didn't know it then. All I knew was that I'd been duped and I was angry. Anyway, Friday afternoon I drove around your neighborhood looking for Caroline, and I insisted she go out with me tonight. I told her she owed me a date, but Chrissy, it was all a big mistake." Bart smiled at her again, and Chrissy felt that same melting sensation she always felt when he smiled at her like that. "Chrissy, there's only one girl I want to date, and she's a crazy farm girl from Iowa who makes me laugh and feel good."

"Do I do that?" Chrissy asked.

."You do." Bart laughed lightly. "You make me feel happy and carefree and . . ."

"But what about your mother?" Chrissy interrupted. She hated to bring up the subject, but she had to know.

"What about my mother?" Bart asked curiously.

"All those things she said about me not being the right type of girl for you and stuff like that."

Bart blushed. "I'm sorry you had to hear that. I didn't realize my mother and I were talking so loud."

"You weren't." Chrissy grinned sheepishly. "I sort of listened at the door," she confessed.

He stared at her for a moment in surprise, then threw back his head and laughed. "Chrissy, you're really something else!" He sobered and looked at her thoughtfully. "Chrissy, you have to understand something about my parents. They're pretty old-fashioned in a lot of ways. They believe in proper breeding and bloodlines. They really don't mean to be snobs—that's just the way they are. I try to do what I can to please them. I go to the school they think is the best, and I'm friendly with the people at the country club. But I draw the line when they tell me who to date." He smiled at her and took her hands in his. "Chrissy, I still want to see you, and if you still want to see me, then I think that's all that's really important, don't you?"

Chrissy nodded, her heart bursting with happiness.

"Now," Bart continued. "You remember that little hamburger drive-in we went to after the Shakespeare reading, when you lost your shoe? How about going there now? You can tell me all about Danbury, Iowa, over hamburgers and shakes."

"Sounds great!" Chrissy jumped up off the sofa and grinned at him in anticipation. "Let's go!"

Bart shook his head in amusement. "Chrissy, they served you shoeless before, but somehow I think they'd frown on you showing up at the drive-in in your bathrobe!"

Chrissy clapped her hand to her forehead. "Holy Mazoly, I forgot all about my robe. Wait here and I'll go change!" She ran to the bedroom, humming a medley of all the love songs she could think of.

"Chrissy . . ." Caroline sat up on her bed and looked at her cousin anxiously. "Chrissy, we need to talk."

"We can't talk now," Chrissy said, quickly peeling off the robe and pulling on a pair of jeans and an ovesized sweater. "Bart and I are going out for a little while."

"Chrissy, please . . . it will just take a minute."

"Okay," Chrissy agreed, hearing the anxiety in Caroline's voice. She sat down on the edge of her bed and faced Caroline.

"First of all, about tonight with Bart . . ."

"Forget it," Chrissy said.

"You aren't mad at me?" Caroline asked hesitantly.

"No, I'm not mad," Chrissy grinned. "Especially since I found out Bart took you to the ballet. You'd accept a date with Dracula if he had tickets to the ballet!"

Caroline smiled in relief, but she still had more to say. "I also owe you an apology about last night. I said some pretty horrible things to you." She looked down at the carpet.

Chrissy got up from her bed and sat down next to her cousin. "I was pretty mad last night after you said those things," she admitted. "But this afternoon I got to thinking, and I realized you were right." Caroline started to protest, but Chrissy stopped her. "Let me finish, Cara. You were right to be mad about your clothes. I've been careless with your things and that isn't right. And the dancing . . ."

This time Caroline did interrupt. "Chrissy, if you want to dance, that's fine with me. Seeing you so excited about ballet just reminded me of how much I used to enjoy it, and I took out my resentment on you."

Chrissy giggled. "Cara, I really don't want to dance anymore. At first I was dancing because I wanted to show Bart, then when he broke up with me, dancing was the only thing that took my mind off him. Honestly, Cara, you must have been super-dedicated to take those classes for so many years." Chrissy looked at Caroline in open admiration.

"What do you mean?" Caroline asked.

"I've got muscles hurting where I didn't even

know I had muscles!" Chrissy exclaimed dramatically.

For a moment the two cousins merely looked at each other.

"Friends again?" Caroline asked with a small smile.

"Always!" Chrissy answered, giving her cousin a big hug. "And now I'd better get out of here before Bart thinks I've forgotten him." She jumped up and headed for the door, pausing as Caroline called her name.

"I'll be glad to help you write that letter to Colorado University. You know, the one asking about scholarships," Caroline offered.

"You really mean it?" Caroline nodded. "You're really the greatest, Cara." Chrissy's smile lit up the room like a brilliant ray of sunshine, then she was gone.

Caroline walked over the bedroom window and watched as Bart and Chrissy got into his car and drove off. With a contented sigh, she got out a piece of her stationery. How could she ever describe the latest escapade she had shared with Chrissy? Caroline nibbled on the end of her pencil, then began to write:

Dear Luke,
   It's been a really wild few weeks. You see, it all started with a blind date . . .

Here's a sneak preview of *It's My Turn*, book number fourteen in the continuing SUGAR & SPICE series from Ivy Books.

"To be or not to be an astronaut!" Chrissy exclaimed, gesturing dramatically. She observed the effect in the mirror and shook her head. "Nah!" she commented. "What do I know about astronauts? I even feel dizzy looking down from the top of a tall building."

My subject for the senior speech must be something I can talk about, she decided. *I can't talk about nuclear physics or even the situation in the Middle East. I've got to think of things I do know something about. . . .*

"The need for conservation on the California coastline, by Christina Madden," she announced.

Again she shook her head. *There's no point in making a speech on that. All the kids at school are for conservation. Besides, just tagging a few seals doesn't make me an expert.* She looked at her reflection critically, taking her long, ash-blond hair and sweeping it experimentally up into a bun on top of her head. She reached out and put a pair of sunglasses on the end of her nose. "How I split the atom, by Doctor Christina Madden," she said. "Well, it was easy. I just picked up a hammer, held the atom very steadily in place and went wham!" As she said "wham" she gestured wildly and the lamp went flying off the dressing table, taking with it the little silver dish in which Caroline kept barrettes, earrings, and any other little knickknacks.

"Whoops!" Chrissy said, kneeling down to inspect the lamp. Luckily it was still in one piece. She was just putting it back in its place when she heard the front door slam.

"Chrissy? Are you home? Where are you—I've got something exciting to tell you!" Her cousin Caroline yelled down the hall, impatient to tell Chrissy her fabulous news. Miss Peters had stopped her after government class that day and had asked her if she'd thought about entering the senior speech contest.

"In the bedroom!" Chrissy called, hastily scooping Caroline's things back into the dish. Before she could put them all back, however, Caroline had flung open the door.

"Chrissy? What in the world are you doing?" Caroline asked. "I thought I heard voices as I came up the steps. Is someone else in here—and what are my barrettes doing all over the floor?"

Chrissy hastily picked up the last of the barrettes and put the dish back on the table. "I was just practicing in front of the mirror," she said.

"Practicing what, dare I ask?" Caroline said with a grin.

"My speech," Chrissy said. "I thought I might enter the senior speech contest. Wouldn't it be great if I won and got to speak at graduation? I can't wait until my mother tells everyone back in Danbury that I'm giving a speech to thousands of important people in a real auditorium!"

"You're thinking of entering the senior speech contest?" Caroline stammered.

"What's wrong with that?" Chrissy asked.

"Er. . . nothing, nothing at all, except that . . . "

"Except that you don't think I'm smart enough to do it?" Chrissy demanded.

"No, it's not that," Caroline stammered, clearly uncomfortable under Chrissy's questioning stare. "I just had no idea . . . I mean, I didn't think you'd ever consider entering a contest like this."

"You thought I wouldn't have a chance of winning?" Chrissy asked. "Well, you're right, on my own I wouldn't have a chance." She got to her feet and beamed excitedly at Caroline. "But you've got to help me, Cara. I know I'm not sophisticated and intellectual like a lot of the kids here. I know the speech will have to be fantastic to win, so I'm going to need your brain power, okay?"

"Chrissy," Caroline said, glaring at her cousin, "You take a lot for granted. You always think that I'm going to help you with everything, even though you know I have very little time for myself as it is. I remember helping you to get dates with cute boys, to get picked for plays, to cook exotic dinners, but I don't remember your helping me very much."

"Of course not," Chrissy said, looking shocked. "You don't need help. You already know how to behave and how to dance and the right thing to say. . . . Besides, the one time I did decide to help you, by getting you together with a boy I thought you liked, you didn't appreciate it one bit."

"That's because you got the wrong boy, dummy," Caroline said with a smile. Then she became serious again. "But had it occurred to you that I might want to enter this speech contest myself?" she asked.

Chrissy grinned. "I can't see you wanting to stand up in front of three thousand people. You—the famous human clam? You hate that sort of thing. I'm the one who likes to be noticed, not you, so we'll make it a team effort, okay? You provide the great ideas and I'll deliver them!"

"And you get credit for both?" Caroline asked, on the verge of losing her self-control.

"Of course not," Chrissy said. "I'll do the sort of thing they do on the Oscars: 'I'd like to thank my wonderful cousin Caroline for making today possible for me—without her help I'd never be standing here at this moment.' How's that?"

"Have you considered the fact that you have to win the contest first before you can do your Oscar routine?" Caroline asked. "What were you thinking of giving a speech on? It has to be something pretty special. 'My school memories, by Chrissy Madden' *is not* going to do it."

"I know that," Chrissy said. "I have several ideas: I thought that maybe conservation might be a good topic, because I've been studying about saving whales and I helped tag those seals last year. Or I could talk about preserving our heritage and bring in how we saved that park from being turned into a parking lot!"

"But Chrissy, I . . . " Caroline began when Chrissy cut her off again.

"I know—you're going to say that's probably too trivial and maybe you're right. It was only a little park. I need something on a grander scale for a speech like this. That's why I need your great brain. Come up with a sizzling topic for me, Cara. You know the sort of thing—controversial, but not too controversial. Sexy, but not too sexy. Funny, but not too funny. Get the picture?"

"Oh sure," Caroline said dryly. "You want me to create the perfect speech for you in the spare time that I don't have. You don't have to take two advanced-placement exams in the next couple of weeks. All you have to do is keep breathing until you graduate."

Chrissy's face fell. "Are you saying you won't do it for me?" she asked, her voice trembling. "I was relying on you, Cara. You've always pulled me through every crisis. I don't want you to write the whole thing—just come up with the topic and get me started. Please Cara . . . pretty please with sugar on top?" She peered into Caroline's face, fluttering her eyelashes hopefully.

"You are a terrible con artist," Caroline said, pushing her away. "I'm going to get myself a snack and then I've got homework to do."

"But you will think about it, won't you, Cara?" Chrissy begged. "We cousins have got to stick together." She turned to watch Caroline walk away and the thought suddenly struck her. "By the way—what was it you wanted to tell me about? You were excited about something, weren't you? Was it good news?"

"It was nothing," Caroline said, not bothering to look around. "Nothing at all."

ABOUT THE AUTHOR

Janet Quin-Harkin is the author of more than forty books for young adults, including the best-selling *Ten-Boy Summer* and *On Our Own*, its sequel series. Ms. Quin-Harkin lives just outside of San Francisco with her husband, three teenage daughters, and one son.